Starmont Popular Fiction #2
ISSN 0895-9323

The
Eighth Green Man
(and Other Strange Folk)
edited by
Robert E. Weinberg

all best!

Starmont House, Inc.
1989

"The Cavern" by Manly Wade Wellman. Copyright © 1938 by Popular Fiction Publishing Co. for *Weird Tales*, September 1938. Reprinted by permission of Karl Edward Wagner, Literary Executor for Manly Wade Wellman.

"The Norn" by Lireve Monet. Copyright © 1936 by Popular Fiction Publishing Co. for *Weird Tales*, February 1936. Reprinted by permission of Jean Eileen Murphy.

"The Eighth Green Man" by G.G. Pendarves. Copyright © 1928 by Popular Fiction Publishing Co. for *Weird Tales*, March 1928. Reprinted by permission of Weird Tales Ltd.

"The Night Wire" by H.F. Arnold. Copyright © 1926 by Popular Fiction Publishing Co. for *Weird Tales*, September 1926. Reprinted by permission of Weird Tales Ltd.

"The House of the Worm" by Mearle Prout. Copyright © 1933 by Popular Fiction Publishing Co. for *Weird Tales*, October 1933. Reprinted by permission of Weird Tales Ltd.

"The Gray Death" by Loual B. Sugarman. Copyright © 1923 by Rural Publications for *Weird Tales*, June 1923. Reprinted by permission of Weird Tales Ltd.

"His Brother's Keeper" by Major George Fielding Eliot. Copyright © 1931 by Popular Fiction Publishing Co. for *Weird Tales*, September 1931. Reprinted by permission of Weird Tales Ltd.

"The Dead Wagon" by Greye La Spina. Copyright © 1927 by Popular Fiction Publishing Co. for *Weird Tales*, September 1927. Reprinted by permission of Weird Tales Ltd.

"The Floor Above" by M.L. Humphries. Copyright © 1923 by Rural Publications for *Weird Tales*, May 1923. Reprinted by permission of Weird Tales Ltd.

"The Wolf–Woman" by Bassett Morgan. Copyright © 1927 by Popular Fiction Publishing Co. for *Weird Tales*, September 1927. Reprinted by permission of Weird Tales Ltd.

Library of Congress Cataloging-in-Publication Data

The Eighth green man and other strange folk / Robert E. Weinberg,
    editor.
        p. cm. -- (Starmont popular fiction ; #2)
        ISBN 1-55742-067-X : -- $19.95 ISBN 1-557-42-066-1 (pbk. : $9.95)
        1. Horror tales, American. 2. American fiction--20th century.
        I. Weinberg, Robert E. II. Series
PS648.H6E34 1989
813'.0873808 -- dc20   89-34754
                                                        CIP

CONTENTS

Introduction
The Eighth Green Man
and
Other Strange Folk

The past twenty years have seen a huge revival of interest in horror and supernatural fiction. The number of novels and short story collections published easily surpasses that of any other time. At present, every month sees ten or more new horror novels appear in paperback, and several more in hardcover. Horror magazines and fanzines continue to print scores of new short stories by an entire new generation of horror fiction authors.

However, as is often the case when such a boom takes place, a great deal of the material being published today is less than spectacular. If two words were to be chosen to describe the short horror fiction being written at present, one word would have to be "vague" and the other "gory."

The major trend in short horror fiction is towards ambiguous stories that leave the reader feeling somewhat uneasy—often queasy—after finishing the tale, and not exactly sure what took place. Too often, storytelling has been sacrificed in the attempt to set a mood. Good authors can do this without much problem, and many fine stories are appearing today that evoke a strong feeling of horror even if the reader is left puzzled. However, too many stories published today only leave the reader puzzled, without arousing any other emotion.

Excessive violence and detailed descriptions of mutilations do not make a horror story, and oftentimes their use merely sickens the reader for no good purpose. Writers forced to resort to such details for shock purposes have forgotten that even horror stories are meant to entertain.

Following that thread of reasoning, this collection has been assembled to provide an entertaining group of horror and weird fiction stories that also feature strong plotting without excessive gore. At the same time, an attempt has been made to select obscure stories from the legendary pulp magazine, *Weird Tales*, that otherwise might never see print—or that were published in long out-of-print hardcover collections that are virtually impossible to find today.

Because stories by most of the "name" writers for *Weird Tales* have been reprinted again and again, there are no stories by H.P. Lovecraft, Robert E. Howard, or Clark Ashton Smith in this volume. Instead, rescued from crumbling pulp pages are stories by the lesser regulars of the magazine—authors like Everil Worrell, G.G. Pendarves, Bassett Morgan, and Manly Wade Wellman.

While Lovecraft and Howard were extremely important to the success of the magazine, they did not appear in every issue. The second-string regulars were the authors whose work kept *Weird Tales* on a regular schedule.

And, while every magazine depended on its regular cast of authors—newcomers and infrequent contributors also played an important role in the life of fiction magazines. *Weird Tales* featured a large number of stories by authors whose names only ever appeared once on the contents page.

Several such stories by one-time and extremely infrequent contributors are reprinted in this book.

Their names are forgotten today, but people like Loual Sugarman and Major George Fielding Eliot also helped make *Weird Tales* "The Unique Magazine."

Welcome, then, to this collection of rare stories by the lesser known and the forgotten, assembled from the pages of a magazine long gone. The horrors here are not as modern as in books today—but just as frightening. Come, spend a night with the Eighth Green Man and the other equally strange and frightening characters who dwell within these pages.

Robert Weinberg
Oak Forest, Illinois

The
Eighth
Green
Man

G.G. Pendarves

G.G. Pendarves

G.G. Pendarves *had a total of nineteen stories published in* Weird Tales *and this, by far, was her most popular contribution. It was reprinted twice, in 1937 and in 1952. As in many of Pendarves' (a pen-name for English authoress Gladys Gordon Trenery) stories, the narrator evidences a thorough knowledge of the dark side of occult lore. Unavailable in book form for years, "The Eighth Green Man" remains one of the classics of occult horror fiction.*

The Eighth Green Man
G.G. Pendarves

I

"Dangerous road, huh!" Nicholas Birkett slowed down and frowned at the battered old sign-post. "I'll take a chance anyhow!"

"I should try another road," I said abruptly.

"But this one leads right down to the valley, and will save at least ten miles round."

"It's a dangerous road—very dangerous," I answered, with the conviction growing fast within me that the sign-post gave only a faint inkling of the deadly peril it guarded..

Birkett stared at me, his big brown hands resting on the steering-wheel. "What d'ye know about the road, anyhow?" he asked, his round blue eyes blank with amazement. "You've never been this way in your life before!"

I hesitated. My name is famous in more than one continent as that of an explorer, and I had recently achieved an expedition across the Sahara Desert which had added immensely to my fame. In fact, it was my lecture on this expedition, given in New York, that had brought about my friendship with Nicholas Birkett. He had introduced himself and carried me off for a stay with him at his country estate in Connecticut, in a whirlwind of enthusiastic interest and admiration.

How could I make my companion understand the shuddering fear that gripped me? I—Raoul Suliman d'Abre—to whom the face of Death was as familiar as my own.

But it was not Death that confronted us on that road marked "Dangerous"...something far less kind and merciful!

Not for nothing am I the son of a French soldier and an Arab woman! Not for nothing was I born in Algeria and grew up amidst the mysteries and magic of Africa. Not for nothing have I learnt in pain and terror that the walls of this visible world are frail and thin—too frail, too thin, alas! For there are times—there are places when the barrier is broken . . . when monstrous unspeakable Evil enters and dwells familiarly amongst us!

"Well!" My companion grew impatient, and began to move the car's nose toward the road on our left.

"I'm sorry," I answered. "The truth is . . . it's a bit difficult to explain . . . but I have my reasons—very strong reasons—for not wishing to go down this particular road. I know—don't ask me how—that it's horribly dangerous. It would a madness—a sin to take that way!"

"But look here, old chap, you can't mean that you . . . that . . . that you're only imagining things about it?"

His face was quite laughable in its astonishment.

I was frightfully embarrassed. How explain to such a rank materialist as Nicholas Birkett that instinct alone warned me against that road? How make a man so insensitive and practical believe in any danger he could not see or handle? He believed in neither God nor Devil! He had only a passionate belief in himself, his wealth, his business acumen, and above all, the physical perfection that went to make his life easy and pleasant.

"There are so many things you do not understand," I said slowly. "I am too old a campaigner to be ashamed of acknowledging that there are some dangers I think it foolhardy to face. This road is one of them!"

"But what in thunder do you know of the damned road?" Birkett's big fresh-colored face turned a brick-red in his angry impatience. Then he cooled down suddenly and put a heavy hand on my knee. "You're ill, old chap! Touch of malaria, I suppose! Excuse my being so darned hasty!"

I shook my head. "You won't or can't understand me! The truth is that I feel the strongest aversion from that path, and I beg you not to take it."

Birkett looked me in the eye and began to argue. He settled down to it solidly. I had nothing to back my arguments except my intuition, and such flimsy nothings as this he demolished with his big hearty laugh, and a heavy elephantine humor that reduced me to a helpless silence.

Opposition always narrowed Birkett down to one idea, that of proving himself right; and at last I said,

"This is more dangerous for you than for me. I am prepared. . . I know how to guard myself from attack, but you—"

"That settles it," he interrupted, gripping the wheel and shooting forward with a jerk. "I can look after myself." His cheerful bellow echoed hollowly as the car dived into the leafy roadway under a branching archway of trees.

II

Birkett became more and more boisterous in his mirth as we sped along, for the road continued smooth and virtually straight, descending in a gentle slope to the Naugatuck valley.

"Dangerous road!" he said, with a prolonged chuckle. "I'll bet a china orange to a monkey that sign means a good long drink. Look out for an innocent little roadhouse tucked away down here. Dangerous road! I suppose that's the latest way of advertising the stuff!

It was useless to remonstrate, but I noticed many things I didn't like along that broad leafy lane.

No living creature moved there—no bird sang—no stir of wings broke the silence of the listening trees—not even a fly moved across our path.

Behind us we had left a world of life, of movement and color. Here all was green and silent. The dark columns of the tree-trunks shut us in like the massive bars of a prison.

Shadows moved softly across the pale, dusty road ahead; shadows that clustered in strange groups about us; shadows not cast by cloud or sun or moving object in our path, for these shadows had no relation to things natural or human.

I knew them! I knew them, and shuddered to recognize their hateful presence.

"You're a queer fellow, d'Abre," my companion rallied me. "You'd waltz out on a camel to meet a horde of yelling, bloodthirsty ruffians in the desert, and thoroughly enjoy the game. Yet here, in a civilized country, you see danger in a peaceful hillside! You certainly are a wonder!"

"Imshallah!" I murmured under my breath. "It is more wonderful that man can be so blind!"

"Are you muttering curses?" Birkett showed white teeth in a flashing grin at my discomfiture. "I suppose it's the Arab half of you that invents these ghosts and devils. Life in the desert must need a few imaginary excitements. But in this country it needs something more than imagination to produce a really lively sort of devil. Something with a good kick to it."

Suddenly, ahead of us, the trees began to thin out, and we caught a glimpse of a low white building to our left. Birkett was triumphant.

"What did I tell you?' he cried. "Here I am leading you straight to a perfectly good drink, and you sit there babbling of death and disaster!"

He stopped the car before a short flight of mossy steps; from the top of them we stood and looked at the house, glimmering palely in the dusky shade of many tall trees.

A flagged path led from where we stood to the house—a straight white path about fifty yards in length. On each side of it the tall, rank grass, dotted with trees and shrubs, stretched back to the verge of the encroaching wood. And within this spacious, park-like enclosure the distant house looked dwarfed and mean—a sort of fungus sprouting at the foot of the stately trees.

Birkett, undeterred by the menacing gloom of the whole place, cupped his hands about his mouth and gave a joyful shout, which echoed and died into heavy silence once more.

"Not expecting visitors," he grinned. "This is a midnight joint, I'll wager. Come on!"

At that moment we saw a sign at our elbow—a freshly painted sign—the lettering in a vivid luminous green on a black ground. It said: "THE SEVEN GREEN MEN."

III

"Seven Green Men, hey! Don't see 'em," said Birkett, moving up the pathway. I followed, looking round intently, every nerve in me sending to my brain its warning thrill of naked, overwhelming terror crouching on every hand, ready to spring, ready to destroy us body and soul.

Then suddenly I saw them—and my heart gave a great leap in my body! They faced us as we approached the house, their grim silhouettes sharp and distinct against the white roadhouse behind.

The Seven Green Men!

"Gee!" said Birkett. "Will you look at those trees? Seven Green Men! What d'you think about that?"

In two stiff rows before the house they stood, each one cut and trimmed to the height of a tall man. Their foliage was dense and unlike that of any tree or shrub I had seen in all my wanderings. A few feet away, their overlapping leaves gave all the illusion of metal, and seven tall warriors seemed to stand in rank before us, their armor green with age and disuse.

Each figure faced the west, presenting its left side to us; each bared head was that of a man shaved to the scalp, each profile was cut with marvelous cunning, and each was distinct and characteristic; the one thing in common was the eyelid, which in every profile appeared closed in sleep.

And when I say sleep, I mean to say just that.

They could awaken, those Seven Green Men! They could awaken to life and action; their roots were not planted in the kindly earth, but thrust down deep into very hell itself.

"The Seven Green Men! Well, what d'you think of that for an idea?" And my companion planted his feet firmly apart, clasped his hands behind his broad back, and gazed in puzzled admiration at the trees. "Some gardener here, d'Abre! I'd like to have a word with him. Wonder if he'd come and do a bit of work for me. A few of these green fellows would look fine in my own place. Beats me how the faces are cut so differently; must need trimming every day! Yes, I'll say that's some gardener!"

I put my hand on his arm.

"Don't you—can't you see they're not just trees? Come away while there's time, Birkett." And I tried to draw him back from those cursed green men, who, even in sleep, seemed to be watching my resistance to them with sardonic interest. "This place is horrible . . . foul, I tell you!"

"I came for a drink, and if these green fellows can't produce it, I'll pull their noses for them!" His laugh rang and echoed in that silent place. As it died, the door of the inn was opened quickly and a man stood on its threshold.

For a long moment the three of us stood looking at each other, and my blood turned to ice as I saw the great massive figure of the innkeeper. Most smooth and urbane he was, that smiling devil—most punctilious and deferential in manner as he summed us both up, gaged our characters, our powers of resistance, our usefulness to him in the vast scheme of his infernal design.

He came down the flagged path toward us, passing through the stiff, silent rank of the seven green men—four on one side of the path, three on the other.

"Good morning, sirs, good morning! How can I serve you?" His high, whispering voice was a shock; it seemed indecent issuing from that gigantic frame, and I saw from Birkett's quick frown that it grated on him too.

"If you've got a drink wet enough to quench my thirst, I'd be mighty glad,"   answered my friend, rather gruffly.   "And about lunch . . . we might try what your green men can do for us!"

Our host gave a long snickering laugh, and glanced back at the seven trees as though inviting them to share the joke.

He bowed repeatedly. "No doubt of that, sir! No doubt of that! If you'll come this way, we'll give you some of the best—the very best." His whisper broke on a high squeak. "Lunch will be served in ten minutes."

I put a desperate hand on Birkett's arm as he began to follow in the wake of the innkeeper.

"Not past them, not past them!" I urged in a low voice. "Look at them now!"

As we approached, the trees seemed to quiver and ripple as though some inner force stirred within their leafy forms, and from each lifted eyelid a sudden flickering glance gleamed and vanished.

Beneath my hand I felt Birkett's involuntary start, but he shook me off impatiently. "Go back, if you like, d'Abre! You'll get me imagining as crazy things as you do, soon." And he stalked on to the house.

IV

"Enter, enter, sirs! My house is honored!"

Unaccountably, as we passed the threshold my horror gave place to a fierce determination to fight—to resist this monstrous swollen spider greedy to catch his human flies.

Power against power—knowledge against knowledge—I would fight while strength and wisdom remained in me.

I waved away the proffered drink

"No, nothing to drink," I said, watching his smooth pale face pucker at this first check in the game.

"Surely, sir, you will drink! You will not refuse to pledge the luck of my house! You are a great man—a great leader of men, that is written in your eyes! It is a privilege to serve so distinquished a guest."

His obsequious whispers sickened me, and I gathered my resources inwardly to meet the assault he was making on my will.

When I refused not only to drink, but to taste a mouthful of the unique lunch provided, a sudden vicious anger flickered in his pale, cold eyes.

"I regret that my poor fare does not please you, sir," he said, his voice like the sound of dry leaves blown before a storm.

"It is better for me that I do not eat," I answer curtly, my eyes meeting his as our wills clashed.

For a long, terrible minute the world dropped from under me; existence narrowed down to those malicious eyes which held mine. I held on with all the desperation of a drowning man tossing in a dark sea of icy waters—torn, buffeted, despairing, at the mercy of incalculable power.

With hideous, intolerable effort I met the attack, and by the mercy of Allah I won at last; for the creature turned from me and smoothly covered his defeat by attending very solicitously to Birkett's needs.

I relaxed, sick and trembling with the price of victory.

I had fought many strange battles in my life; for in the East, the Unknown is a force to be recognized, not laughed at and despised as in the West. Yet of all my encounters, this one was the deadliest, this evil, smiling Thing the strongest I had known in any land or place.

Must Birkett's strength go to feed this insatiable foe who fattened on the race of men?

I shuddered as I watched him sitting there, eating, drinking, laughing with his host; his whole mind bent on the pleasure of the moment, his will relaxed, his brain asleep; while the creature at his side served him with hateful, smiling ease, watching with cool, complacent eye as his victim let down his barriers one by one.

In his annoyance with my behavior, Birkett prolonged the meal as much as possible, ignoring me as I sat smoking and watching our host as intently as he watched us.

Anxiously I wondered what the next move in this horrible cat-and-mouse game would be; but it was not until Birkett rose from the table at last that the enemy showed his hand.

"It's a pity you can't be here on Friday night, sir! You'd be just the one to appreciate it. One of our gala nights—in fact the best night in the year at the Seven Green Men. You'd have a meal worth remembering that night. But I'm afraid they wouldn't let you in on it."

"Why not?" demanded Birkett, instantly aggressive.

"I beg your pardon, sir, but you see it's a very special night indeed. There's a very select society in this neighborhood; I don't suppose you've as much as heard of it: The Sons of Enoch."

"Never heard of 'em." Birkett's tone implied that had they been worth knowing, he would have heard of them. "Who are they? Those seven green chaps you keep in the grounds—eh?"

A cold light flashed in the innkeeper's eyes; and my own heart stood still, for the flippant remark had been nearer the truth than Birkett guessed.

"It's a society that was founded centuries ago, sir. Started in Germany in a little place on the Rhine, run by some old monks. There are members in every country in the world now. This one in America is the last one to be formed, but it's going strong, sir, very strong!"

"They why the devil haven't I been told of it before?"

"Why should you know of all the hole-and-corner clubs that exist?" I interposed. The innkeeper was probing Birkett's weakest part. How well—oh, how truly the smiling, smooth-spoken devil had summed up my poor blundering friend!

"It'll be a society run for the Great Unwashed!" I continued. "You'd be a laughing stock in the neighborhood if it got out that you were mixed up with any sort of scum of that sort!"

"There is much that your great travels have not taught you, sir," answered the innkeeper, his sibilant speech savage as a snake's hiss. "The members of this club are those who stand so high, that as I said, I fear they would not consent to admit you even once to their company."

"Damn it all!" Birkett interrupted irritably. "I'd like to know any fellows out here who refuse to meet me. And who are you, curse you, to judge who can be members or not?"

Our host bowed, and I caught the mocking smile of his thin lips, as the fish rose so readily to his bait.

I poured ridicule on the proposition and did all I could do to turn Birkett aside, but to no avail. Opposition, as always, goaded him to incredible heights of obstinacy; and now, half drunk and wholly in the hands of that subtle devil who had measured him so accurately, the poor fellow fairly galloped into the trap set for him.

It ended with a promise on our host's part to do all in his power to persuade the Sons of Enoch to receive Birkett and perhaps make him a member of their ancient society.

"Friday night then, sir! About 11 o'clock the meeting will start, and there's a midnight supper to follow. Of course I'll do my best for you, but I doubt if you'll be allowed to join."

"Don't worry," was Birkett's valedictory remark, "I'll become one of the Sons of Enoch on Friday, or I'll hound your rotten society out of existence. You'll see, my jolly old innkeeper, you'll see!"

And as we left the grounds, passing once more the Seven Green Men, their leaves rustled with a dry crackle that was the counterpart of the innkeeper's hateful, whispering voice.

V

Our drive homeward was at first distinctly unpleasant. Birkett chose to take my behavior as a personal insult, and, being at a quarrelsome stage of his intoxication, he kept up a muttered commentary: "...insulting a decent old bird like that... best lunch ever had...damned if I won't...Sons of Enoch...what's going to stop me ...be a Son of Enoch...damned interfering fellow, d'Abre!..."

He insisted on driving himself, and took such a roundabout way that it was two hours when we saw New Haven in the distance. Birkett was sober by this time and rather ashamed of his treatment of a guest.

He insisted on pulling up at another little roadhouse, The Brown Owl, run by a New England farmer he wanted me to meet.

"You'll like the old chap, d'Abre!" he assured me, eager to make amends for his lapse. "He's a great old man, and can put up a decent meal. Come on, you must be starving."

I was thankful to make the acquaintance of both old Paxton and his fried chicken . . . and Birkett's restored geniality made me hopeful that after all he might not prove obdurate about repeating his visit to the Seven Green Men.

Old Paxton sat with us later on his porch, and gradually the talk veered round to our late excursion. The old farmer's face changed to a mask of horror.

"The Seven Green Men! Seven, did you say? My God!...oh, my God!"

My pulses leaped at the loathing and fear in his voice; and Birkett brought his tilted chair down on the floor with a crash. Staring hard at Paxton, he said aggressively, "That's what I said! Seven! It's a perfectly good number; lots of people think it's lucky."

But the farmer was blind and deaf to everything—his mind gripped by some paralyzing thought.

"Seven of them now...seven! And no one believed what I told 'em! Poor soul, whoever it is! Seven now. Seven Green Men in that accursed garden!"

He was so overcome that he just sat there, saying the same things over and over again.

Suddenly, however, he got to his feet and hobbled stiffly across the veranda, beckoning us to follow. He led us down the steps to his peach orchard behind the house, and pointed to a figure shambling about among the trees.

"See him . . .see him!" Paxton's voice was hoarse and shaken. "That's my only son, all that's left of him."

The awkward figure drew nearer, approaching us at a loping run, and Birkett and I instinctively drew back. It was an imbecile, a slobbering, revolting wreck of humanity with squinting eyes and loose mouth, and a big, heavy frame on which the massive head rolled sickeningly.

He fell at Paxton's feet, and the old man's shaking hand patted the rough head pressed against his knees.

"My only son, sirs!"

We were horribly abashed and afraid to look at old Paxton's working features.

"He was the Sixth Green Man . . . and may the Lord have mercy on his soul!"

The poor afflicted creature shambled off, and we went back to the house in silence.

Awkwardly avoiding the farmer's eye, Birkett paid the reckoning and started for his car, when Paxton laid a detaining hand on his arm.

"I see you don't believe me, sir! No one will believe! If they had done so, that house would be burnt to the ground, and those trees . . . those green devils with it! It's they who steal the soul out of a man, and leave him like my son!"

"Yes," I answered. "I understand what you mean."

Paxton peered with tear-dimmed eyes into my face.

"You understand! Then I tell you they're still at their fiend's game! My son was the Sixth . . . the Sixth of those Green Men! Now there are Seven! They're still at it!"

VI

"How about staying on here and having another swim when the moon rises?" I said, apparently absorbed in making my old briar pipe draw properly, but in reality waiting with overwhelming anxiety for Birkett's reply.

It was Friday evening, and no word had passed between us during the week of the Seven Green Men, or Birkett's decision about tonight.

He was sitting there on the rocks at my side, his big body stretched out in the sun in lazy enjoyment, his half closed eyes fixed on the blue outltine of Long Island on the opposite horizon.

"Well, how about it?" I repeated, after a long silence.

He rolled over regarding me mockingly.

"Anxious nurse skilfully tries to divert her charge from his naughty little plan! No use, d'Abre; I've made up my mind about tonight, and nothing's going to stop me."

I bit savagely on my pipe-stem, and frowned at an offending gull which wheeled to and fro over the lapping water at our feet.

As easily could a six-months-old baby digest and assimilate raw meat as could Birkett's intellect grasp anything save the obvious; nevertheless I was impelled to make another attempt to break down the ramparts of his self-sufficient obstinacy.

But I failed, of course. The world of thought and imagination and intuition was unknown and therefore non-existent to him. The idea of any form of life, not classified and labeled, not belonging to the animal or vegetable kingdom, was simply a joke to him.

And old Paxton's outbursts he dismissed as lightly as the rest of my arguments.

"My dear chap, everyone knows the poor old fellow's half mad himself with trouble. The boy was a wild harum-scarum creature, always into mischief and difficulties. No doubt he did go to a midnight supper at the Seven Green Men. But what's that got to do with it? You might as well say if you got sunstroke, for instance, that old Paxton's fried chicken caused it!"

VII

"You don't mean to say that you're coming too?' asked Birkett, when, about 10:30 that night, I followed him out of doors to his waiting car.

"But of course!" I answered lightly. "You don't put me down as a coward as well as a believer in fairy-tales, do you?"

"You're a sport, anyhow, d'Abre!" he said warmly. "And I'm very glad you're coming to see for yourself what one of our midnight joints is like. It'll be a new experience for you."

"And for you," I said under my breath, as he started the engine and passed out from his dim-perfumed garden to the dusty white highroad beyond.

A full moon sailed serenely among silvery banks of cloud above us; and in the quiet night river and valley, rocky hillside and dense forest had the sharp, strange outlines of a woodcut.

All too soon we reached the warning sign, "Dangerous Road," and passed from a silver, sleeping earth to the stagnant gloom of that tunnellike highway.

But hateful as it was, I could have wished that road would never end, rather than bring us, as inevitably it did, to that ominous green-and-black sign of our destination.

The sound of a deep rhythmic chant greeted us as we went up the steps, and we saw that the roadhouse was lit from end to end. Not with the mellow, welcoming radiance of lamp or candle, but with strange quivering fires of blue and green, which flickered to and fro in mad haste past every window of the inn.

"Some illumination!" remarked Birkett. "Looks like the real thing to me! Do you hear the Sons of Enoch practicing their nursery rhymes! Coming, boys!", he roared cheerfully. "I'll join in the chorus!"

As for myself, I could only stare at the moonlit garden in horror, for my worst fears were realized, and I knew just how much I had dreaded this moment when I saw that the seven tall trees—those sinister deviltrees—were gone!

Then I turned, to see the huge bulk of the innkeeper close behind us, his head thrown back in silent laughter, his eyes smoldering fires above the ugly, cavernous mouth.

Birkett turned too, at my exclamation, and drew his heavy eyebrows together in a frown.

"What the devil do you mean by creeping up to us like that?" he demanded angrily.

Still laughing, the innkeeper came forward and put his hand familiarly on my friend's arm. "By the Black Goat of Zarem," he muttered, "you are come in a good hour. The Sons of Enoch wait to receive you—I myself have seen to it—and tonight you shall both learn the high mysteries of their ancient order!"

"Look here, my fine fellow," said Birkett, "what the deuce do you mean by crowing so loud? I've got to meet these queer minstrels of yours before I decide to join them."

From the house came a great rolling burst of song, a tremendous chant with an earth-shaking rhythm that was like the shock of battle. The ground rocked beneath us; gathering clouds shut out the face of the watchful moon; a sudden fury of wind shook the massed trees about the house and grounds until they moaned and hissed like lost souls, tossing their crests in impotent agony.

In the lull which followed, Birkett's voice came to me, low and strangely subdued: "You're right, d'Arbe! This place is unhealthful. Let's quit." And he moved back toward the steps.

But the creature at our side laughed again and raised his hand. Instantly the grounds were full of shifting lights, moving about us—hemming us in, revealing dim outlines of swollen, monstrous bodies, and bloated features which thrust forward sickeningly to gloat and peer at Birkett and me.

The former's shuddering disgust brought them closer and closer upon us, and I whispered hastily, "Face them! Face them! Stamp on them if you can; they only advance as you retreat!"

Our host's pale, smiling face darkened as he saw our resolution, and a wave of his hand reduced the garden to empty darkness once more.

"So!" he hissed. "I regret that my efforts to amuse you are not appreciated. If I had thought you a coward"—turning to Birkett—"I would not have suggested that you come tonight. The Sons of Enoch have no room for a coward in their midst!"

"Coward!" Birkett's voice rose to a bellow at the insult, and in reaction from his horror. "Why, you grinning white-faced ape! Say that again and I'll smash you until you're uglier than your filthy friends here. No more of your conjuring tricks! Get on to the house and show me these precious Sons of yours!"

I put my hand on his arm, but the blind anger to which the innkeeper had purposely roused him made him incapable of thought or reason, and he shook me off angrily.

Poor Birkett! Ignorant, undisciplined, and entirely at the mercy of his appetites and emotions—what chance had he in his fatuous immaturity against our enemy? I followed him despairingly. His last chance of escape was gone if he entered that house of his own free will.

"The trees are gone!" I said in a loud voice, pulling Birkett back, and pointing. "Ask him where the trees are gone!"

But as I spoke, the outlines of the Seven Green Men rose quivering in the dimness of the garden. Unsubstantial, unreal, more shadows cast by the magic of the Master who walked by our side, they stood there again in their stiff, silent ranks!

"What the deuce are you talking about?" growled Birkett. "Come on! I'll see this thing through now, if I'm hanged for it."

I caught the quick malice of the innkeeper's glance, and shivered. Birkett was a lump of dough for this fiend's molding, and my blood ran cold at the thought of the ordeal to come.

VIII

Over the threshold of the house! . . . and with one step we passed the last barrier between ourselves and the unseen.

No familiar walls stood around us, no roof above us. We were in the vast outer darkness which knows neither time nor space.

I drew an Arab knife from its sheath—a blade sharpened on the sacred stone of the Kaaba, and more potent here than all the weapons in an arsenal.

Birkett took my wrists in his big grasp and pointed vehemently with his other hand. In any other place I could have smiled at his bewilderment; now, I could only wish with intense bitterness that his intellect equaled his obstinacy. Even now he discredited his higher instincts; even here he was trying to measure the vast spaces of eternity with his little foot-rule of earthbound dimensions.

Our host stood before us—smiling, urbane as ever; and at his side the Seven Green Men towered, bareheaded and armor-clad, confronting us in ominous silence, their eyes devouring hells of sick desire!

"My brothers!" At the whispered word, Birkett stiffened at my side and his grip on my arm tightened.

"My brothers, the Sons of Enoch, wait to receive you to their fellowship. You shall be initiated as they have been. You shall share their secrets, their sufferings, their toil. You have come here of your own free will . . . now you shall know no will but mine. Your existence shall be my existence! Your being my being! Your strength my strength! What is the Word?"

The Seven Green Men turned toward him.

"The Word is thy Will, Master of Life and Death!"

"Receive, then, the baptism of the initiate!" came the whispered command.

Birkett made a stiff step forward, but I restrained him with frantic hands.

"No! No!" I cried hoarsely. "Resist... resist him."

He smiled vacantly at me, then turned his glazed eyes in the direction of the whispering voice again.

"No faith defends you... no knowledge guides you... no wisdom inspires you. Son of Enoch, receive your baptism!"

I drew my dagger and flung myself in front of Birkett as he brushed hastily past me and advanced toward the smiling Master. But the Seven Green Men ringed us in, stretching out stiff arms in a wide circle, machinelike, obedient to the hissing commands of their superior.

I leapt forward, and with a cutting slash of my knife got free and strode up to the devil who smiled, and smiled, and smiled!

"Power is mine!" I said, steadying my voice with hideous effort. "I know you... I name you... Gaffarel!"

IX

In the gray chill of dawn I stood once more before the house of the Seven Green Men. The dark woods waited silent and watchful, and the house itself was shuttered, and barred, and silent too.

I looked around wildly as thought and memory returned. Birkett . . . Birkett, where was he?

Then I saw the trees! The devil trees, stiff, grotesque in their armor, silhouetted against the white, blank face of the roadhouse behind.

The Seven Green Men!

Seven... no... there were eight men now! I counted them! My voice broke with a cry as I counted and recounted those frightful trees.

Eight!

As I stood there sobbing the words... eight... eight... eight over and over, with terror mounting in my brain, the narrow door of the inn opened slowly, and a figure shambled out and down the path toward me.

A big, heavy figure that gibbered at me as it came, pouring out a stream of meaningless words until it reached my feet, where it collapsed in the long dewy grass.

It was Birkett—Nicholas Birkett! I recognized the horrible travesty of my friend at last, and crept away from him into the forest, for I was very sick.

The sign was freshly painted as we passed it coming out, much later, for it was long before I could bring myself to touch Birkett, and take him out to the waiting car.

The sign was freshly painted as we passed . . . and the livid green words ran:

"THE EIGHT GREEN MEN."

The
Night
Wire

H. F. Arnold

H. F. Arnold

In a survey conducted by SF historian Sam Moskowitz, of the most popular stories ever published in Weird Tales, *"The Night Wire" placed forty-first. This achievement is even more noteworthy considering the extreme brevity of the tale and that it was published as a filler in the rear of the September 1926 issue when it first appeared. Despite its dated setting, "The Night Wire" is a story not easily forgotten.*

The Night Wire

H. F. Arnold

"New York, September 30 CP Flash

Ambassador Holliwell died here today. The end came suddenly as the ambassador was alone in his study. . . ."

There is something ungodly about these night wire jobs. You sit up here on the top floor of a skyscraper and listen into the whispers of a civilization. New York, London, Calcutta, Bombay, Singapore—they're your next-door neighbors after the street lights go dim and the world has gone to sleep.

Along in the quiet hours between two and four, the receiving operators doze over their sounders and the news comes in. Fires and disasters and suicides. Murders, crowds, catastrophies. Sometimes an earthquake with a casualty list as long as your arm. The night wire man takes it down almost in his sleep, picking it off on his typewriter with one finger.

Once in a long time you prick up your ears and listen. You've heard of some one you knew in Singapore, Halifax or Paris, long ago. Maybe they've been promoted, but more probably they've been murdered or drowned. Perhaps they just decided to quit and took some bizarre way out. Made it interesting enough to get in the news.

But that doesn't happen often. Most of the time you sit and doze and tap, tap on your tyupewriter and wish you were home in bed.

Sometimes, though, queer things happen. One did the other night, and I haven't got over it yet. I wish I could.

You see, I handle the night manager's desk in a western seaport town; what the name is, doesn't matter.

There is, or rather was, only one night operator on my staff, a fellow named John Morgan, about forty years of age, I should say, and a sober, hard-working sort.

He was one of the best operators I ever knew, what is known as a "double" man. That means he could handle two instruments at once and type the stories on different typewriters at the same time. He was one of the three men I ever knew who could do it consistently, hour after hour, and never make a mistake.

Generally, we used only one wire at night, but sometimes, when it was late and the news was coming fast, the Chicago and Denver stations would open a second wire, and then Morgan would do his stuff. He was a wizard, a mechanical automatic wizard which functioned marvelously but was without imagination.

On the night of the sixteenth he complained of feeling tired. It was the first and last time I had ever heard him say a word about himself, and I had known him for three years.

It was just three o'clock and we were running only one wire. I was nodding over reports at my desk and not paying much attention to him, when he spoke.

"Jim," he said, "does it feel close in here to you?"

"Why, no, John," I answered, "but I'll open a window if you like."

"Never mind," he said. "I reckon I'm just a little tired."

That was all that was said, and I went on working. Every ten minutes or so I would walk over and take a pile of copy that had stacked up neatly beside the typewriter as the messages were printed out in triplicate.

It must have been twenty minutes after he spoke that I noticed he had opened up the other wire and was using both typewriters. I thought it was a little unusual, as there was nothing very "hot" coming in. On my next trip I picked up the copy from both machines and took it back to my desk to sort out the duplicates.

The first wire was running out the usual sort of stuff and I just looked over it hurriedly.

Then I turned to the second pile of copy. I remembered it particularly because the story was from a town I had never heard of: "Xebico". Here is the dispatch. I saved a duplicate of it from our files:

"Xebico, Sept. 16   CP BULLETIN

"The heaviest mist in the history of the city settled over the town at 4 o'clock yesterday afternoon. All traffic has stopped and the mist hangs like a pall over everything. Lights of ordinary intensity fail to pierce the fog, which is constantly growing heavier.

"Scientists here are unable to agree as to the cause, and the local weather bureau states that the like has never occurred before in the history of the city.

"At 7 P.M. last night municipal authorities...

(more)"

That was all there was. Nothing out of the ordinary at a bureau headquarters, but, as I say, I noticed the story because of the name of the town.

It must have been fifteen minutes later that I went over for another batch of copy. Morgan was slumped down in his chair and had switched his green electric light shade so that the gleam missed his eyes and hit only the top of the two typewriters.

Only the usual stuff was in the righthand pile, but the lefthand batch carried another story from Xebico. All press dispatches come in "takes"—that is, parts of many stories are strung along together, perhaps with but a few paragraphs of each coming through at a time. This second story was marked "add fog." Here is the copy:

"At 7 P.M. the fog had increased noticeably. All lights were now invisible and the town was shrouded in pitch darkness.

"As a peculiarity of the phenomenon, the fog is accompanied by a sickly odor, comparable to nothing yet experienced here."

Below that in customary press fashion was the hour, 3:27, and the initials of the operator, JM.

There was only one other story in the pile from the second wire. Here it is:

"2nd add Xebico Fog

"Accounts as to the origin of the mist differ greatly. Among the most unusual is that of the sexton of the local church, who groped his way to headquarters in a hysterical condition and declared that the fog originated in the village churchyard.

"It was first visible as a soft gray blanket clinging to the earth above the graves,' he stated. 'Then it began to rise, higher and higher. A subterranean breeze seemed to blow it in billows, which split up and then joined together again.

"'Fog phantoms, writhing in anguish, twisted the mist into queer forms and figures. And then, in the very thick midst of the mass, something moved.

"'I turned and ran from the accursed spot. Behind me I heard screams from the houses bordering on the graveyard.'

"Although the sexton's story is generally discredited, a party has left to investigate. Immediately after telling his story, the sexton collapsed and is now in a local hospital, unconscious."

Queer story, wasn't it. Not that we aren't used to it, for a lot of unusual stories come in over the wire. But for some reason or other, perhaps because it was so quiet that night, the report of the fog made a great impression on me.

It was almost with dread that I went over to the waiting piles of copy. Morgan did not move, and the only sound in the room was the tap-tap of the sounders. It was ominous, nerve-racking.

There was another story from Xebico in the pile of copy. I seized on it anxiously.

"New Lead Xebico Fog CP

"The rescue party which went out at 11 P.M. to investigate a weird story of the origin of a fog which, since late yesterday, has shrouded the city in darkness, has failed to return. Another and larger party has been dispatched.

"Meanwhile the fog has, if possible, grown heavier. It seeps through the cracks in the doors and fills the atmosphere with a depressing odor of decay. It is oppressive, terrifying, bearing with it a subtle impression of things long dead.

"Residents of the city have left their homes and gathered in the local church, where the priests are holding services of prayer. The scene is beyond description. Grown folk and children are alike terrified and many are almost beside themselves with fear.

"Amid the wisps of vapor which partly veil the church auditorium, an old priest is praying for the welfare of his flock. They alternately wail and cross themselves.

"From the outskirts of the city may be heard cries of unknown voices. They echo through the fog in queer uncadenced minor keys. The sounds resemble nothing so much as wind whistling through a gigantic tunnel. But the night is calm and there is no wind. The second rescue party . . . (more)"

I am a calm man and never in a dozen years spent with the wires have been known to become excited, but despite myself I rose from my chair and walked to the window.

Could I be mistaken, or far down in the canyons of the city beneath me did I see a faint trace of fog? Pshaw! It was all imagination.

In the pressroom the click of the sounders seemed to have raised the tempo of their tune. Morgan alone had not stirred from his chair. His head sunk between his shoulders, he tapped the dispatches out on the typewriters with one finger of each hand.

He looked asleep, but no; endlessly, efficiently, the two machines rattled off line after line, as relentlessly and effortlessly as death itself. There was something about the monotonous movement of the typewriter keys that fascinated me. I walked over and stood behind his chair, reading over his shoulder the type as it came into being, word by word.

Ah, here was another:

"Flash Xebico CP

"There will be no more bulletins from this office. The impossible has happened. No messages have come into this room for twenty minutes. We are cut off from the outside and even the streets below us.

"I will stay with the wire until the end.

"It is the end, indeed. Since 4 P.M. yesterday the fog has hung over the city. Following reports from the sexton of the local church, two rescue parties were sent out to investigate conditions on the outskirts of the city. Neither party has ever returned nor was any word received from them. It is quite certain now that they will never return.

"From my instrument I can gaze down on the city beneath me. From the position of this room on the thirteenth floor, nearly the entire city can be seen. Now I can see only a thick blanket of blackness where customarily are lights and life.

"I fear greatly that the wailing cries heard constantly from the outskirts of the city are the death cries of the inhabitants. They are constantly increasing in volume and are approaching the center of the city.

"The fog yet hangs over everything. If possible, it is even heavier than before, but the conditions have changed. Instead of an opaque impenetrable wall of odorous vapor, there now swirls and writhes a shapeless mass in contortions of almost human agony. Now and again the mass parts and I catch a brief glimpse of the streets below.

"People are running to and fro, screaming in despair. A vast bedlam of sound flies up to my window, and above all is the immense whistling of unseen and unfelt winds.

"The fog has again swept over the city and the whistling is coming closer and closer.

"It is now directly beneath me.

"God! An instant ago the mist opened and I caught a glimpse of the streets below.

"The fog is not simply vapor—it lives! By the side of each moaning and weeping human is a companion figure, an aura of strange and vari-colored hues. How the shapes cling! Each to a living thing!

"The men and women are down. Flat on their faces. The fog figures caress them lovingly. They are kneeling beside them. They are—but I dare not tell it.

"The prone and writhing bodies have been stripped of their clothing. They are being consumed—piecemeal.

"A merciful wall of hot, steamy vapor has swept over the whole scene. I can see no more.

"Beneath me the wall of vapor is changing colors. It seems to be lighted by internal fires. No, it isn't. I have made a mistake. The colors are from above, reflections from the sky.

"Look up! Look up! The whole sky is in flames. Color as yet unseen by man or demon. The flames are moving; they have started to intermix; the colors rearrange themselves. They are so brilliant that my eyes burn, yet they are a long way off.

"Now they have begun to swirl, to circle in and out, twisting in intricate designs and patterns. The lights are racing each with each, a kaleidoscope of unearthly brilliance.

"I have made a discovery. There is nothing harmful in the lights. They radiate force and friendliness, almost cheeriness. But by their very strength, they hurt.

"As I look, they are swinging closer and closer, a million miles at each jump. Millions of miles with the speed of light. Aye, it is light the quintessence of all light. Beneath it the fog melts into a jeweled mist, radiant, rainbow-colored of a thousand varied spectra.

"I can see the streets. Why, they are filled with people! They are all around me. I am enveloped. I..."

The message stopped abruptly. The wire to Xebico was dead. Beneath my eyes in the narrow circle of light from under the green lamp-shade, the black printing no longer spun itself, letter by letter, across the page.

The room seemed filled with a solemn quiet, a silence vaguely impressive, powerful.

I looked down at Morgan. His hands had dropped nervelessly at his sides, while his body had hunched over peculiarly. I turned the lamp-shade back, throwing the light squarely in his face. His eyes were staring, fixed.

Filled with a sudden foreboding, I stepped beside him and called Chicago on the wire. After a second the sounder clicked its answer.

Why? But there was something wrong. Chicago was reporting that Wire Two had not been used throughout the evening.

"Morgan!" I shouted. "Morgan! Wake up, it isn't true. Some one has been hoaxing us. Why . . ." In my eagerness I grasped him by the shoulder.

His body was quite cold. Morgan had been dead for hours. Could it be that his sensitized brain and automatic fingers had continued to record impressions even after the end?

I shall never know, for I shall never again handle the night shift. Search in a world atlas discloses no town of Xebico. Whatever it was that killed John Morgan will forever remain a mystery.

The
House
of the
Worm

Mearle Prout

Mearle Prout

Though Farnsworth Wright, editor of Weird Tales, *rarely expressed opinions contrary to those of his readers, he did mention from time to time stories he felt had not received proper acclaim. In response to a reader's question, Wright named "The House of the Worm" as one of those neglected masterpieces. Prout was an Oklahoma author, who contributed only four stories to "The Unique Magazine." All were excellent work, but "The House of the Worm" stands as his masterpiece of horror.*

The House of the Worm

Mearle Prout

But see, amid the mimic rout
A crawling shape intrude!
A blood-red thing that writhes from out
The scenic solitude!
It writhes!—it writhes!—with mortal pangs
The mimes become its food
And the angels sob at vermin fangs
In human gore imbued.
                    —Edgar Allan Poe

For hours I had sat at my study table, trying in vain to feel and transmit to paper the sensations of a criminal in the death-house. You know how one may strive for hours—even days—to attain a desired effect, and then feel a sudden swift rhythm, and know he has found it? But how often, as though Fate herself intervened, does interruption come and mar, if not cover completely, the road which for a moment gleamed straight and white! So it was with me.

Scarcely had I lifted my hands to the keys when my fellow-roomer, who had long been bent quietly over a magazine, said, quietly enough, "That moon—I wonder if even it really exists!"

I turned sharply. Fred was standing at the window, looking with a singularly rapt attention into the darkenss.

Curious, I rose and went to him, and followed his gaze into the night. There was the moon, a little past its full, but still nearly round, standing like a great red shield close above the tree-tops, yet real enough....

Something in the strangeness of my friend's behavior prevented the irritation which his unfortunate interruption would ordi-
narily have caused.

"Just why did you say that?" I asked, after a moment's hesita-
tion.

'Shamefacedly he laughed, half apologetic. "I'm sorry I spoke
aloud," he said. "I was only thinking of a bizarre theory I ran
across in a story."

"About the moon?"

"No. Just an ordinary ghost story of the type you write. *While
Pan Walks* is its name, and there was nothing in it about the
moon."

He looked again at the ruddy globe, now lighting the darkened street below with a pale, tenuous light. Then he spoke:
"You know, Art, that idea has taken hold of me; perhaps there is
something to it after all. . . ."

Theories of the bizarre have always enthralled Fred, as they
always hold a romantic appeal for me. And so, while he revolved
his latest fancy in his mind, I waited expectantly.

"Art," he began at last, "do you believe that old story about
thoughts becoming realities? I mean, thoughts of men having a
physical manifestation?"

I reflected a moment, before giving way to a slight chuckle.
"Once," I answered, "a young man said to Carlyle that he had
decided to accept the material world as a reality; to which the older
man only replied, 'Egad, you'd better!' . . . Yes," I continued, "I've
often run across the theory, but . . ."

"You've missed the point," was the quick rejoinder. "Accept
your physical world, and what do you have?—Something that was
created by God! And how do we know that all creation has
stopped? Perhaps even we. . . ."

He moved to a book-shelf, and in a moment returned, dusting
off a thick old leather-bound volume.

"I first encountered the idea here," he said, as he thumbed
the yellowed pages, "but it was not until that bit of fiction pressed
it into my mind that I thought of it seriously. Listen:

"'The Bible says, "In the beginning God created the heavens
and the earth." From what did He create it? Obviously, it was created by thought, imagery, force of will if you please. The Bible

further says: "So God created man in His own image." Does this not mean that man has all the attributes of the Almighty, only upon a smaller scale? Surely, then, if the mind of God in its omnipotence could create the entire universe, the mind of man, being made in the image of God, and being his counterpart on eath, could in the same way, if infinitely smaller in degree, create things of its own will.

"'For example, the old gods of the dawn-world. Who can say that they did not exist in reality, being created by man? And, once created, how can we tell whether they will not develop into something to harass and destroy, beyond all control of their creators? *If this be true, then the only way to destroy them is to cease to believe.* Thus it is that the old gods died when man's faith turned from them to Christianity'."

He was silent a moment, watching me as I stood musing.

"Strange where such thoughts can led a person," I said. "How are we to know which things are real and which are fancies—racial fantasies, I mean, common in all of us. I think I see what you mean when you wondered if the moon were real."

"But imagine," said my companion, "a group of people, a cult, all thinking the same thoughts, worshipping the same imaginary figure. What might not happen, if their fanaticism were such that they thought and felt deeply? A physical manifestation, alien to those of us who did not believe...."

And so the discussion continued. And when at last we finally slept, the moon which prompted it all was hovering near the zenith, sending its cold rays upon a world of hard physical reality.

Next morning we both arose early—Fred to go back to his prosaic work as a bank clerk, I to place myself belatedly before my typewriter. After the diversion of the night before, I found that I was able to work out the bothersome scene with little difficulty, and that evening I mailed the finished and revised manuscript.

When my friend came in he spoke calmly of our conversation the night before, even admitting that he had come to consider the theory a rank bit of metaphysics.

Not quite so calmly did he speak of the hunting-trip which he suggested. Romantic fellow that he was, his job at the bank was sheer drudgery, and any escape was rare good fortune. I, too, with my work out of the way and my mind clear, was doubly delighted at the prospect.

"I'd like to shoot some squirrels," I agreed. "And I know a good place. Can you leave tomorrow?"

"Yes, tomorrow; my vacation starts then," he replied. "But for a long time I've wanted to go back to my old stamping-grounds. It's not so very far—only a little over a hundred miles, and"—he looked at me in apology for differing with my plans—"in Sacrament Wood there are more squirrels than you ever saw."

And so it was agreed.

Sacrament Wood is an anomaly. Three or four miles wide and twice as long, it fills the whole of a peculiar valley, a rift, as it were, in the rugged topography of the higher Ozarks. No stream flows through it, there is nothing to suggest a normal valley; it is merely there, by sheer physical presence defying all questions. Grim, tree-flecked mountains hem it in on every side, as though seeking by their own ruggedness to compensate this spot of gentleness and serenity. And here lies the peculiarity: though the mountains around here are all inhabited—sparsely, of course, through necessity—the valley of the wood, with every indication of a wonderful fertility, has never felt the plow; and the tall, smooth forest of scented oak has never known the ax of the woodman.

I too had known Sacrament Wood; it was generally recognized as a sportsman's paradise, and twice, long before, I had hunted there. But that was so long ago that I had all but forgotten, and now I was truly grateful to have been reminded of it again. For if there is a single place in the world where squirrels grow faster than they can be shot, it is Sacrament Wood.

It was midafternoon when we finally wound up the last mountain trail to stop at last in a small clearing. A tiny shanty with clapboard roof stood as ornament beside the road, and behind it a bent figure in faded overalls was chopping the withered stalks of cotton."

"That would be old Zeke," confided my companion, his eyes shining with even this reminder of childhood. "Hallo!" he shouted, stepping to the ground.

The old mountaineer straightened, and wrinkled his face in recognition. He stood thus a moment, until my companion inquired as to the hunting; then his eyes grew dull again. He shook his head dumbly.

"Ain't no hunting now, boys. Everything is dead. Sacrament Wood is dead."

"Dead!" I cried. "Impossible! Why is it dead?"

I knew in a moment that I had spoken without tact. The mountaineer has no information to give one who expresses a desire for it—much less an outlander who shows incredulity.

The old man turned back to his work. "Ain't no hunting now," he repeated, and furiously attacked a stalk of cotton.

So obviously dismissed, we could not remain longer. "Old Zeke has lived too long alone," confided Fred as we moved away. "All mountaineers get that way sooner or later."

We continued. The road stretched ahead for some distance along the level top. And then, as we started the rough descent, Sacrament Wood burst full upon our view, clothed as I had never before seen it. Bright red, yellow, and brown mingled together in splashes of beauty as the massive trees put on their autumnal dress. Almost miniature it appeared to us from our lookout, shimmering like a mountain lake in the dry heat of early fall.

Night comes early in the deep valley of Sacrament Wood. The sun was just resting on the high peak in the west as we entered the forest and made camp. But long after comparative darkness had come over us, the mountain down which we had come was illuminated a soft gold.

We sat over our pipes in the gathering dusk. It was deeply peaceful, there in the darkening wood, and yet Fred and I were unnaturally silent, perhaps having the same thoughts. Why were the massive trees so early shorn of leaves? Why had the birds ceased to sing?

A cheery fire soon dispelled our fears. We were again the two hunters, rejoicing in our freedom and our anticipation. At least, I was. Fred, however, somewhat overcame my feeling of security.

"Art, whatever the cause, we must admit that Sacrament Wood is dead. Why, man, those trees are not getting ready for dormance; they are dead. Why haven't we heard birds? Bluejays used to keep this place in a continual uproar. And where did I get the feeling I had as we entered here? Art, I am sensitive to these things. I can *feel* a graveyard in the darkest night; and that is how I felt as I came here—as if I was entering a graveyard. I *know*, I tell you!"

"I felt it, too," I answered. "But all that is gone now. The fire changes things."

"Yes, the fire changes things. Hear that moaning in the trees? You think that is the wind? Well, you're wrong, I tell you. That is not the wind. Something not human is suffering; maybe the fire hurts it."

I laughed, uncomfortably enough. "Come," I said, "you'll be giving me the jimmies, too. I felt the same way you did; I even smelt an odor, but the old man just had us upset. That's all. The fire has changed things. It's all right now."

"Yes," he said, "it's all right now."

For all his nervousness, Fred was the first to sleep that night. We heaped the fire high before turning in, and I lay for a long while and watched the leaping flames. And I thought about the fire.

"Fire is clean," I said to myself, as though directed from without. "Fire is clean; fire is life. The very life of our bodies is preserved by oxidation. Yes, without fire there would be no cleanness in the world."

But I too must have dropped off, for when I was awakened by a low moan the fire was dead. The wood was quiet; not a whisper or rustle of leaves disturbed the heavy stillness of the night. And then I sensed the odor. . . . Once sensed, it grew and grew until the air seemed heavy, even massive, with the inertia of it, seemed to press itself into the ground through sheer weight. It eddied and swirled in sickening waves of smell. It was the odor of death, and putridity.

I heard another moan.

"Fred," I called, my voice catching in my throat.

The only answer was a deeper moan.

I grasped his arm, and—my fingers sank in the bloated flesh as into a rotting corpse! The skin burst like an over-ripe berry, and slime flowed over my hand and dripped from my fingers.

Overcome with horror, I struck a light; and under the tiny flare I saw for a moment—his face! Purple, bloated, the crawling flesh nearly covered his staring eyes; white worms swarmed his puffed body, exuded squirming from his nostrils, and fell upon his livid lips. The foul stench grew stronger; so thick was it that my tortured lungs cried out for relief. Then, with a shriek of terror, I cast the lighted match from me, and threw myself into the bed, and buried my face in the pillow.

How long I lay there, sick, trembling, overcome with nausea, I do not know. But I slowly became aware of a rushing sound in the tree-tops. Great limbs creaked and groaned; the trunks themselves seemed to crack in agony. I looked up and saw a ruddy light reflected about us. And like a crash of thunder came the thought into my brain:

"Fire is clean; fire is life. Without fire there would be no cleanness in the world."

And at this command I rose, and grasped everything within reach, and cast it upon the dying flames. Was I mistaken, or was the odor of death really less? I hauled wood, and heaped the fire high. Fortunate indeed that the match I had thrown had fallen in the already sere leaves!

When next I thought of my companion the roaring blaze was leaping fifteen feet in the air. Slowly I turned, expecting to see a corpse weltering in a miasma of filth, and saw—a man calmly sleeping! His face was flushed, his hands still slightly swollen; but he was clean! He breathed. Could I, I asked, have dreamed of death, and the odor of death? Could I have dreamed the *worms?*

I awoke him, and waited.

He half looked at me, and then, gazing at the fire, gave a cry of ecstasy. A light of bliss shone for a moment in his eyes, as in a young child first staring at the mystery of cleansing flame; and then, as realization came, this too faded into a look of terror and loathing.

"The worms!" he cried. "The maggots! The odor came, and with it the worms. And I awoke. Just as the fire died. . . . I couldn't cry out. The worms came—I don't know whence; from nowhere, perhaps. They came, and they crawled, and they ate. And the smell came with them! It just appeared, as did the worms, from out of thin air! It just—became. Then—death!—I died, I tell you—I rotted—I rotted, and the worms—the maggots—they ate... I am *dead,* I say! *Dead!* Or should be!" He covered his face with his hands.

How we lived out the night without going mad, I do not know. All through the long hours we kept the fire burning high; and all through the night the lofty trees moaned back their mortal agony. The rotting death did not return; in some strange way the fire kept us clean of it, and fought it back. But our brains felt, and dimly comprehended, the noisome evil floundering in the darkness, and the pain which our immunity gave this devilish forest. I could not understand why Fred had so easily fallen a victim to the death, while I remained whole. He tried to explain that his brain was more receptive, more sensitive.

"Sensitive to what?" I asked.

But he did not know.

Dawn came at last, sweeping westward before it the web of darkness. From across the forest, and around us on all sides, the giant trees rustled in pain, suggesting the gnashing of millions of anguished teeth. And over the ridge to eastward came the smiling sun.

Never was a day so long in coming, and never so welcome its arrival. In a half-hour our belongings were gathered, and we quickly drove to the open road.

"Fred, you remember our conversation of a couple of evenings ago? I asked my companion, after some time of silence. "I'm wondering whether that couldn't apply here."

"Meaning that we were the victims of—hallucination? Then how do you account for this?" He raised his sleeve above his elbow, showing his arm. How well did I remember it! For there, under curling skin and red as a brand, was the print of my hand!

"I sensed, not felt, you grip me last night," said Fred. "There is our evidence."

"Yes," I answered, slowly. "We've got lots to think of, you and I."

And we rode together in silence.

When we reached home, it was not yet noon, but the brightness of the day had already wrought wonders with our perspective. I think that the human mind, far from being a curse, is the most merciful thing in the world. We live on a quiet, sheltered island of ignorance, and from the single current flowing by our shores we visualize the vastness of the black seas around us, and see—simplicity and safety. And yet, if only a portion of the crosscurrents and whirling vortexes of mystery and chaos would be revealed to our consciousness, we should immediately go insane.

The wound on Fred's arm healed quickly; in a week not even a scar remained. But we were changed. We had seen the crosscurrent, and—we knew. By daylight a swift recollection often brought nausea; and the nights, even with the lights left burning, were rife with horror. Our very lives seemed bound into the events of one night.

Yet, even so, I was not prepared for the shock I felt when, one night nearly a month later, Fred burst into the room, his face livid.

"Read this," he said in a husky whisper, and extended a crumpled newspaper to my hand. I reached for it, read where he had pointed.

MOUNTAINEER DIES

Ezekiel Whipple, lone mountaineer, aged 64, was found dead in his cabin yesterday by neighbors.

The post-mortem revealed a terrible state of putrefaction; medical men aver that death could not have occurred less than two weeks ago.

The examination by the coroner revealed no sign of foul play, yet local forces for law and order are working upon what may yet be a valuable clue. Jesse Layton, a near neighbor and close friend of the aged bachelor, states that he visited and held conversation with him the day preceding; and it is upon this statement that anticipation of possible arrest is based.

"God!" I cried. "Does it mean. . . ."

"Yes! It's spreading—whatever it is. It's reaching out, crawling over the mountains. God knows to where it may finally extend."

"No. It is not a disease. It is alive. It's alive, Art! I tell you, I felt it; I heard it. I think it tried to talk to me."

For us there was no sleep that night. Every moment of our half-forgotten experience was relived a thousand times, every horror amplified by the darkness and our fears. We wanted to flee to some far country, to leave far behind us the terror we had felt. We wanted to stay and fight to destroy the destroyer. We wanted to plan; but—hateful thought—how could we plan to fight—nothing? We were as helpless as the old mountaineer.

And so, torn by these conflicting desires, we did what was to be expected—precisely nothing. We might even have slipped back into the even tenor of our lives had not news dispatches showed still further spread, and more death.

Eventually, of course, we told our story. But lowered glances and obvious embarrassment told us too well how little we were believed. Indeed, who could expect normal people of the year 1933, with normal experiences, to believe the obviously impossible? And so, to save ourselves, we talked no more, but watched in dread from the sidelines the slow, implacable growth.

It was midwinter before the first town fell in the way of the expanding circle. Only a mountain village of half a hundred inhabitants; but the death came upon them one cold winter night— late at night, for there were no escapes—and smothered all in their beds. And when the next day visitors found and reported them, there was described the same terrible advanced state of putrefaction that had been present in all the other cases.

Then the world, apathetic always, began to believe. But, even so, they sought the easiest, the most natural explanation, and refused to recognize the possibilities we had outlined to them. Some new plague, they said, is threatening us, is ravaging our hill country. We will move away. . . . A few moved. But the optimists, trusting all to the physicians, stayed on. And we, scarce knowing why, stayed on with them.

Yes, the world was waking to the danger. The plague became one of the most popular topics of conversation. Revivalists predicted the end of the world. And the physicians, as usual, set to work. Doctors swarmed the infected district, in fear of personal safety examined the swollen corpses, and found—the bacteria of decay, and—the worms. They warned the natives to leave the surrounding country; and then, to avoid panic, they added encouragement.

"We have an inkling of the truth," they said, after the best manner of the detective agency. "It is hoped that we may soon isolate the deadly bacterium, and produce an immunizing serum."

And the world believed. . . . I, too, half believed, and even dared to hope.

"It is a plague," I said, "some strange new plague that is killing the country. We were there, first of all."

But "No," said Fred. "It is not a plague. I was there; I felt it; it talked to me It is Black Magic, I tell you! What we need is, not medicine, but medicine men."

And I—I half believed him, too!

*   *   *

Spring came, and the encroaching menace had expanded to a circle ten miles in radius, with a point in the wood as a center. Slow enough, to be sure, but seemingly irresistible. . . . The quiet, lethal march of the disease, the *death,* as it was called, still remained a mystery—and a fear. And as week after week fled by with no good tidings from the physicians and men of science there assembled, my doubts grew stronger. Why, I asked, if it were a plague, did it never strike its victims during the day? What disease could strike down all life alike, whether animal or vegetable?

"Fred," I said one day, "they can't stand fire—if you are right. We'll burn the wood. We'll take kerosene. We'll burn the wood, and if you are right, the thing will die."

His face brightened. "Yes," he said, "we'll burn the wood, and—the thing will die. Fire saved me: I know it; you know it. Fire could never cure a disease; it could never make normal trees whisper and groan, and crack in agony. We'll burn the wood, and the thing will die."

So we said, and so we believed. And we set to work.

Four barrels of kerosene we took, and tapers, and torches. And on a clear, cold day in early March we set out in the truck. The wind snapped bitterly out of the north; our hands grew blue with chill in the open cab. But it was a clean cold. Before its pure sharpness, it was almost impossible to believe that we were heading toward filth and a barren country of death. And, still low in the east, the sun sent its bright yellow shafts over the already budding trees.

It was still early morning when we arrived at the edge of the slowly enlarging circle of death. Here the last victim, only a day or so earlier, had met his end. Yet, even without this last to tell us of its nearness, we could have judged by the absence of all life. The tiny buds we had noted earlier were absent; the trees remained dry and cold as in the dead of winter.

Why did not the people of the region heed the warnings and move? True, most of them had done so. But a few old mountaineers remained—and died one by one.

We drove on, up the rocky, precipitous trail, leaving the bustle and safety of the normal world behind us. A faint stench assailed my nostrils—the odor of death. It grew and it grew. Fred was pale; and, for that matter, so was I. Pale—and weak.

"We'll light a torch," I said. "Perhaps this odor will die."

We lit a torch in the brightness of the day, then drove on.

Once we passed a pig-sty: white bones lay under the sun; the flesh was decayed and eaten away entirely.

The sun was still bright, but weak, in some strange way. It shone doubtfully, vacillating, as if there were a partial eclipse.

But the valley was near. We passed the last mountain, passed the falling cabin of the mountaineer who was the first to die. We started the descent.

Sacrament Wood lay below us, not fresh and green as I had seen it first, years before, nor yet flashing with color as on our last trip the autumn before. It was cold, and obscured. A black cloud lay over it, a blanket of darkness, a rolling mist like that which is said to obscure the River Styx. It covered the region of death like a heavy shroud, and hid it from our probing eyes. Could I have been mistaken, or did I hear a broad whisper rising from the unhallowed wood of the holy name? Or did I feel something I could not hear?

But in one respect I could not be wrong. It was growing dark. The farther we moved down the rocky trail, the deeper we descended into this stronghold of death, the paler became the sun, the more obscured our passage.

"Fred," I said in a low voice, "they are hiding the sun. They are destroying the light. The wood will be dark."

"Yes," he answered. "The light hurts them. I could feel their pain and agony that morning as the sun rose; they can not kill in the day. But now they are stronger, and are hiding the sun itself. The light hurts them, and they are destroying it."

We lit another torch and drove on.

When we reached the wood, the darkness had deepened, the almost palpable murk had thickened until the day had become as a moonlight night. But it was not a silver night. The sun was red; red as blood, shining on the accursed forest. Great red rings surrounded it, like the red rings of sleeplessness surrounding a diseased eye. No, the sun itself was not clean; it was weak, diseased, powerless as ourselves before the new terror. Its red glow mingled with the crimson of the torches, and lit up the scene around us with the color of blood.

*   *   *

We drove as far as solid ground would permit our passage—barely to the edge of the forest, where the wiry, scraggly growth of cedar and blackjack gave way to the heavy growth of taller, straighter oak. Then we abandoned our conveyance and stepped upon the rotting earth. And at this, more strongly it seemed than before, the stench of rottenneess came over us. We were thankful that all animal matter had decayed entirely away; there only remained the acrid, penetrating odor of decaying plants; disagreeable, and powerfully suggestive to our already sharpened nerves, but endurable. . . . And it was warm, there in the death-ridden floor of the valley. In spite of the season of the year and the absence of the sun's warmth, it was not cold. The heat of decay, of fermentation, overcame the biting winds which occasionally swept down from the surrounding hills.

The trees were dead. Not only dead; they were rotten. Great limbs had crashed to the ground and littered the soggy floor. All smaller branches were gone, but the trees themselves remained upright, their naked limbs stretched like supplicating arms to the heavens as these martyrs of the wood stood waiting. Yet in even these massive trunks the worms crawled—and ate. It was a forest of death, a nightmare, fungous forest that cried out to the invaders, that sobbed in agony at the bright torches, and rocked to and fro in all its unholy rottenness.

Protected by our torches, we were immune to the forces of death that were rampant in the dark reaches of the wood, beyond our flaring light. But while they could not prey upon our bodies, they called, they drew upon our minds. Pictures of horror, of putridity and nightmare thronged our brains. I saw again my comrade as he had lain in his bed, over a half-year before; I thought of the mountain village, and of the three-score victims who had died there in one night.

We did not dare, we knew, to dwell on these things; we would go insane. We hastened to collect a pile of dead limbs. We grasped the dank, rotten things—limbs and branches which broke on lifting, or crumbled to dust bvetween our fingers. At last, however, our heap was piled high with the dryest, the firmest of them, and over all we poured a full barrel of kerosene. And as we lit the vast pile, and watched the flames roar high and higher, a sigh of pain, sorrow and impotent rage swept the field of death.

"The fire hurts them," I said. "While there is fire they can not harm us; the forest will burn, and they will all die."

"But will the forest burn? They have dimmed the sun; they have even dimmed our torches. See! They should be brighter! Would the forest burn of itself, even if thety let it alone? It is damp and rotten, and will not burn. See, our fire is burning out! We have failed."

Yes, we had failed. We were forced to admit it when, after two more trials, we were at last satisfied beyond any doubt that the forest could not be destroyed by fire. Our hearts had been strong with courage, but now fear haunted us, cold perspiration flooded our sick, trembling bodies as we sent the clattering truck hurtling up the rocky trail to safety. Our torches flared in the wind, and left a black trail of smoke behind us as we fled.

But, we promised ourselves, we would come again. We would bring many men, and dynamite. We would find where this thing had its capital, and we would destroy it.

And we tried. But again we failed.

There were no more deaths. Even the most obstinate moved from the stricken country when spring came and revealed the actual presence of the deadly circle. No one could doubt the mute testimony of the dead and dying trees that fell in its grip. Fifty, a hundred or two hundred feet in a night the circle spread; trees that one day were fresh and alive, sprouting with shoots of green, were the next day harsh and yellow. The death never retreated. It advanced during the nights; held its ground during the day. And at night again the fearful march continued.

A condition of terror prevailed over the populations in adjoining districts. The newspapers carried in their columns nothing but blasted hopes. They contained long descriptions of each new advance; long, technical theories of the scientists assembled at the front of battle; but no hope.

We pointed this out to the terror-ridden people, told them that in our idea lay the only chance of victory . We outlined to them our plan, pleaded for their assistance. But "No," they said. "The plague is spreading. It began in the wood, but it is out of the wood now. How would it help to burn the wood now? The world is doomed. Come with us, and live while you can. We must all die."

No, there was no one willing to listen to our plan. And so we went north, where the death, through its unfamiliarity and remoteness, had not yet disrupted society. Here the people, doubtful, hesitant, yet had faith in their men of science, still preserved order, and continued industry. But our idea received no welcome. "We trust the doctors," they said.

And none would come.

"Fred," I told him, "we have not yet failed. We will equip a large truck. No! We will take a tractor. We will do as we said. Take more kerosene, and dynamite; we will destroy it yet!"

It was our last chance; we knew that. If we failed now, the world was indeed doomed. And we knew that every day the death grew stronger, and we worked fast to meet it.

The materials we needed we hauled overland in the truck: more torches, dynamite, eight barrels of kerosene. We even took two guns. And then we loaded all these in an improvised trailer behind the caterpillar, and started out.

The wood was dark now, although it was not yet midday when we entered. Black as a well at midnight was the forest; our torches sent their flickering red a scant twenty feet through the obstinate murk. And through the shivering darkness there reached our ears a vast murmur, as of a million hives of bees.

How we chose a path I do not know; I tried to steer toward the loudest part of the roar, hoping that by so doing we would find the source itself of the scourge. And our going was not difficult. The tractor laid down its endless track, rushing to paste beneath it the dank, rotting wood which littered the forest floor. And from behind, over the smooth track crushed through the forest, lumbered the heavy trailer.

The gaunt, scarred trees, shorn of every limb, stood around us like weird sentinels pointing the way. And, if possible, the scene grew more desolate the farther we proceeded; the creaking trunks standing pole-like seemed more and more rotten; the odor of death around us, not the sickening odor of decay, but the less noxious yet more penetrating smell of rottenness complete, grew even more piercing. And *It* called and drew. From out of the darkness it crept into our brains, moved them, changed them to do its will. We did not know. We only knew that the odor around us no longer nauseated; it became the sweetest of perfumes to our nostrils. We only knew that the fungus-like trees pleased our eyes, seemed to fill and satisfy some long-hidden esthetic need. In my mind there grew a picture of a perfect world: damp, decayed vegetation and succulent flesh—rotting flesh—upon which to feed. Over all the earth, it seemed, this picture extended; and I shouted aloud in ecstasy.

At the half-involuntary shout, something flashed upon me, and I knew that these thoughts were not my own, but were foisted upon me from without. With a shriek, I reached to the torch above and bathed my arms in the living flame; I grasped the taper from its setting and brandished it in my comrade's face. The cleansing pain raced through my veins and nerves; the picture faded, the longing passed away; I was myself again.

Then, suddenly, above the roar from without and the steady beat of our engine, we heard a human chant. I idled the motor, jerked out the gears. Clear on our ears it smote now, a chant in a familiar, yet strangely altered tongue. Life! In this region of death? It was impossible! The chant ceased, and the hum among the poles of trees doubled in intensity. Someone, or something, rose to declaim. I strained my ears to hear, but it was unnecessary; clear and loud through the noisome darkness rose its high semi-chant:

"Mighty is our lord, the Worm. Mightier than all the kings of heaven and of earth is the Worm. The gods create; man plans and builds; but the Worm effaces their handiwork.

"Mighty are the planners and the builders; great their works and their possessions. But at last they must fall heir to a narrow plot of earth; and even that, forsooth, the Worm will take away.

"O Master! On bended knee we give thee all these things! We give unto thee the life of the earth to be thy morsel of food! We give unto thee the earth itself to be thy residence!

"Mighty, oh mighty above all the kings of heaven and of earth is our lord and master, the Worm, to whom Time is naught!"

Sick with horror and repulsion, Fred and I exchanged glances. There was life! God knew what sort, but life, and human! Then, there in that forest of hell, with the odor, sight, and sound of death around us, we smiled! I swear we smiled! We were given a chance to fight; to fight something tangible. I raced the motor, snapped the machine into gear and pushed on.

And one hundred feet farther I stopped, for we were upon the worshippers! Half a hundred of them there were, crouching and kneeling, yes, even wallowing in the putrefaction and filth around them. And the sounds, the cries to which they gave vent as our flaming torches smote full upon their sightless, staring eyes! Only a madman could recall and place upon the printed page the litanies of hate and terror which they flung into our faces. There are vocal qualities peculiar to men, and vocal qualities peculiar to beasts; but nowhere this side of the pit of hell itself can be heard the raucous cries that issued from their straining throats as we grasped our tapers and raced toward them. A few moments only did they stand defiantly in our way; the pain of the unaccustomed light was too much for their sensitive eyes. With shrill shouts of terror they turned and fled. And we looked about us, upon the weltering filth with which we were surrounded, and—smiled again!

For we saw their idol! Not an idol of wood, or stone, or of any clean, normal thing. It was a heaped-up grave! Massive, twenty feet long and half as high, it was covered with rotting bones and limbs of trees. The earth, piled there in the gruesome mound, shivered and heaved as from some foul life within. Then, half buried in filth, we saw the headstone—itself a rotting board, leaning askew in its shallow setting. And on it was carved only the line: *The House of the Worm*.

The house of the worm! A heaped-up grave. And the cult of blackness and death had sought to make of the world one foul grave, and to cover even that with a shroud of darkness!

With a shriek of rage I stamped my foot upon the earth piled there. The crust was thin, so thin that it broke through, and nearly precipitated me headlong into the pit itself; only a violent wrench backward prevented me from falling into the pitching mass of— worms! White, wriggling, the things squirmed there under our blood-red, flaring light, writhed with agony in the exquisite torture brought to them by the presence of cleansing flame. The house of the worm, indeed.

Sick with loathing, we worked madly. The roar of the alien forest had risen to a howl—an eldritch gibber which sang in our ears and drew at our brains as we toiled. We lit more torches, bathed our hands in the flame, and then, in defiance of the malign will, we demolished the quivering heap of earth which had mocked the form of a grave. We planted dynamite. We carried barrel after barrel of fuel, and poured it upon the squirming things, which were already spreading out, rolling like an ocean of filth at our very feet. And then, forgetting the machine which was to take us to safety, I hurled the box of black powder upon them, watched it sink through the mass until out of sight, then applied the torch. And fled.

"Art! The tractor—the rest of the oil we need to light our way out...."

I laughed insanely, and ran on.

Two hundred yards away, we stopped and watched the spectacle. The flames, leaping fifty feet into the air, illumined the forest around us, pushed back the thick unnatural gloom into the heavy darkness behind us. Unseen voices that howled madly and mouthed hysterical gibberish tore at our very souls in their wild pleading; so tangible were they that we felt them pull at our bodies, sway them back and forth with the unholy dance of the rocking trees. From the pit of foulness where the flames danced brightest, a dense cloud of yellow smoke arose; a vast frying sound shrilled through the wood, was echoed back upon us by the blackness around. The tractor was enveloped in flames, the last barrel of oil spouting fire. And then...

There came a deep, heavy-throated roar; the pulpy ground beneath our feet waved and shook; the roaring flames, impelled by an irresistible force beneath them, rose simultaneously into the air, curved out in long sweeping parabolas of lurid flame, and scattered over the moaning forest floor.

The house of the worm was destroyed; and simultaneously with its destruction the howling voices around us died into a heavy-throated whisper of silence. The black mist of darkness above and about shook for a moment like a sable silk, caught groping at us, then rolled back over the ruined trees and revealed—the sun!

The sun, bright in all his noonday glory, burst out full above us, warming our hearts with a golden glow.

"See, Art!" my companion whispered, "the forest is burning! There is nothing now to stop it, and everything will be destroyed."

It was true. From a thousand tiny places flames were rising and spreading, sending queer little creepers of flame to explore for further progress.

We turned, we walked swiftly into the breath of the warm south wind which swept down upon us; we left the growing fire at our backs and moved on. A half-hour later, after we had covered some two miles of fallen forest and odorous wasteland, we paused to look back. The fire had spread over the full width of the valley, and was roaring northward. I thought of the fifty refugees who had fled—also to the north.

"Poor devils!" I said. "But no doubt they are already dead; they could not endure the brightness of the sun for long."

And so ends our story of what is perhaps the greatest single menace that has ever threatened mankind. Science pondered, but could make nothing of it; in fact, it was long before we could evolve an explanation satisfactory even to ourselves.

We had searched vainly through every reference book on the occult, when an old magazine suddenly gave us the clue: it recalled to our minds a half-forgotten conversation which has been reproduced at the beginning of this narrative.

In some strange way, this Cult of the Worm must have organized for the worship of death, and established their headquarters there in the valley. They built the huge grave as a shrine, and by the over-concentration of worship of their fanatical minds, caused a physical manifestation to appear within it as the real result of their thought. And what suggestion of death could be more forceful that its eternal accompaniment—the worms of death and the bacteria of decay? Perhaps their task was lessened by the fact that death is always a reality, and does not need so great concentration of will to produce.

At any rate, from that beginning, that center, they radiated thought-waves strong enough to bring their influence over the region where they were active; and as they grew stronger and stronger, and as their minds grew more and more powerful through the fierce mental concentration, they spread out, and even destroyed light itself. Perhaps they received many recruits, also, to strengthen their ranks, as we ourselves nearly succumbed; perhaps, too, the land once conquered was watched over by spirits invoked to their control, so that no further strength on their part was required to maintain it. That would explain the weird noises heard from all parts of the forest, which persisted even after the worshippers themselves had fled.

And as to their final destruction, I quote a line from the old volume where we first read of the theory: *"If this be true, the only way to destroy it is to cease to believe."*   When the mock grave, their great fetish, was destroyed, the central bonds which held their system together were broken. And when the worshippers themselves perished in the flames, all possibility of a recurrence of the terror died with them.

This is our explanation, and our belief.

The
Gray
Death

Loual B. Sugarman

Loual B. Sugarman

Few of the stories published in the first year of Weird Tales *are worth rereading today. Ideas fresh in 1923 have long since lost their luster. However, dramatic presentation can make even the most familiar plots seem new. Many other stories have appeared in the past sixty years using the same theme as "The Gray Death" but few have ever matched it in presentation.*

The Gray Death

Loual B. Sugarman

Unwaveringly, my guest sustained my perplexed and angry stare. Silently he withstood the battering words I launched at him. He appeared quite unmoved by my reproaches, save for a dull red flush that crept up and flooded his face, as now and then I grew particularly bitter in my tirade.

At length I ceased. It was like hitting into a mass of feathers: there was no resistance to my blows. He had made no attempt to justify himself. After a moment of silence, he spoke his first word since he had entered the room.

"I'm sorry, my friend, sorrier than you can imagine, but—I couldn't help it. I simply could not touch her hand. The shock— so suddenly to come upon her—to see her as she was—I tell you, I forgot myself. Please convey to your wife my most abject apologies, will you? I am sorry, for I know I should have liked her very much. But—now I must go."

"You can't go out in this storm," I answered. "It's out of the question. I'm sorry, too, sorry that you acted as you did—and more than sorry that I spoke to you as I did, just now. But I was angry. Can you blame me? I'd been waiting for this moment ever since I heard from you that you had come back from the Amazon—the moment when you, my best friend, and my wife were to meet. And then—why, damn it, man, I can't understand it! To pull back, to shrink away as you did; even to refuse to take her hand or acknowledge the introduction! It was unbelievably rude. It hurt her, and it hurt me."

"I know it, and that is why I am so very sorry about it all. I can't excuse myself, but I can tell you a story that may explain."

I saw, however, that for some reason he was reluctant to talk.

"You need not," I said. "Let's drop the whole matter, and in the morning you can make your amends to Laura."

Anthony shook his head.

"It's not pleasant to talk about, but that was not my reason for hesitating. I was afraid you would not believe me if I did tell you. Sometimes the truth strains one's credulity too much. But I will tell you. It may do me good to talk about it, and, anyhow, it will explain why I acted as I did.

"Your wife came in just after we entered. She had not yet removed her veil or gloves. They were gray. So was her dress. Her shoes—everything was gray. And she stood there, her hand outstretched—all in that color—a body covered with gray. I can't help shuddering. *I can't stand gray!* It's the color of death. . . . Can your nerves stand the dark?"

I rose and switched off the lights. The room was plunged into darkness, save for the flicker of the flames in the fireplace and the intermittent flashes of lightning. The rain beat through the leafless branches outside with a monotonous, slithering swish and rattled like ghostly fingers against the windows.

"The light makes it hard to talk—of unbelievable things. One needs the darkness to hear of hell."

He paused. The *swir-r-r of* the rain crept into the stillness of the room. My companion sighed. The firelight shone on his face, which floated in the darkness—a disembodied face, grown suddenly haggard.

"A good night for this story, with the wind crying like a lost soul in the night. How I hate that sound! Ah, well!"

There was a moment of silence.

"It was not like this, though, that night when we started up the Amazon. No. Then it was warm and soft, and the stars seemed so near. The air was filled with the scent of a thousand tropical blossoms. They grew rank on the shore.

"There were four of us; two natives, myself and Von Housmann. It is of him I am going to tell you. He was a German—and a good man. A great naturalist, and a true friend. He sucked the poison from my leg once, when a snake had bitten me. I thanked him and said I'd repay him some day. I did—sooner than I had thought—with a bullet! I could not bear to see him suffer!

The man sat gazing into the flames, and I listened to the dripping rain fingering the bare boughs and *tap-tap-tapping* on the roof above.

My friend looked up.

"I was seeing his face in the flames," he said. "God help him!"

"We had traveled for days—weeks—how long does not matter. We had camped and moved on; we had stopped to gather specimens—always deeper into that evil undergrowth. And as we moved on, Von Housmann and I drew closer; one either grows to love or hate in such circumsances, and Sigmund was not the sort of man one would hate. I tell you, I loved that man!

"One day we struck into a new place. We had left the tracks of other expeditions long before. We trekked along, unmindful of the exotic beauty of our surroundings, when I saw our native, who was up ahead, stop short and sniff the air.

"We stopped, too, and then I noticed what the keener, more primitive sense of our guide had detected first.

"It was an odor. A strange odor, indefinable and sickening. It was filled with foreboding—evil. It smelt—*gray!* I can not describe it any other way. It smelt dead. It made me think of decay—decay, and mold, and—ugly things.

"I shuddered. I looked at Von Housmann, and I saw that he, too, had noticed it.

"'What is that smell?' I asked.

"He shook his head.

"'Ach, dot is new. I haf not smelled it before. But—I do not lige it. It iss not goot. Smells iss goot or bat—und dot is not goot. I say, I do not lige dot smell.'

"Neither did I. We went ahead, cautiously now. A curious scent pervaded the air. It puzzled me. Then it struck me: *silence.* Silence, as though the music of the spheres had suddenly been snuffed out. It was the utter cessation of the interminable chirping and chattering of the birds and monkeys and other small animals.

"We had become so accustomed to that multitudinous babel that its absence was disturbing. It was—eery. Yes, that's the word. It made that first impression of lifelessness more intense. Not death, you understand. Even death has in it a thought of life, an element of being. But this was just—lifelessness..

"The gray odor had become so strong that it was well nigh unbearable. Then we saw our guides running back to us. They rebelled. They refused to go beyond the line of trees ahead. They said it was *taboo*.

"That ended it. No promise, no threat, nothing would move them. Do you know what a savage's *taboo* is? It is stronger than death. And this place was *taboo*. So we left them there with our stuff, and Sigmund and I went on alone. We reached the farthest line of trees and stopped on the edge of a clearing.

"I can't describe that sight to you. But I can see it—good God, how I can still see it! Sometimes I wake up in the night with that nightmarish picture in my eyes, and my nostrils filled with that ghoulish stench.

"It was a field of gray; almost, I might have said, a field of *living* gray. And yet it did not give the impression of life. It moved, although there was not a breath of wind; not a leaf on the trees quivered, but that mass of gray wriggled and crawled and undulated as though it were a huge gray shroud thrown over some monstrous jelly-like Thing. And that Thing was writhing and twisting.

"The gray mass extended as far as I could see ahead. To the right the sandy shore of the river stopped it, and to the left and in front of us it terminated at a distance of a few yards away from the trees where a belt of sand intervened.

"I don't know how long we stood there, my friend Von Housmann and I. It fascinated us. At last he spoke.

"'*Heilige Mutter. Was kommt da?* Vot in der name off all dot iss holy do you call dot? Nefer haf I seen such before. Eferyvere I haf traffeled, but nefer haf I seen a sight lige dot. It tell you, it makes my flesh crawl!'

"'It makes me sick to look at it,' I answered. 'It looks like—like living corruption.'

"The old German shook his head. He was baffled. We knew we were looking upon something that no living mortal had ever gazed upon before. And our flesh crawled, as we watched that Thing writhing beneath its blanket of gray.

"We walked slowly and cautiously across the strip of sand to the edge of the gray patch. As I bent over, the pungency of the odor bit into the membrane of my nostrils like an acid, and my eyes smarted.

"And then I saw something that drove all other thoughts from my mind. The mass was a moss-like growth of tiny gray fungi. They were shaped like miniature mushrooms, but out of the top of each grew a countless number of antennae that ceaselessly twisted and writhed in the air. They seemed to be feeling and groping around for something, and it was this incessant movement that gave to the patch that quivering undulation which I had noticed before.

"I stared until my eyes ached. 'What do you make of it?' I asked my friend.

"'*Ach,* I do not know. It iss incombrehensible. I haf never seen such a—a t'ing in my whole, long life. It iss, I should say, some sort off a fungoid growt'. *Ya,* it iss clearly dot. But der species—um, dot iss *not* so clear. Und dose liddle feelers; on a fungus dot iss new—it is unheard off. See, die verdammte t'ings is liger lifting fingers; dey svay und tvist lige dey was feeling for somet'ings, not? I am egseedingly curious. And I am baffled—und, my friendt, I do not lige dot.'

"Impatiently, he reached out a stick he was carrying, a newly cut, stout cudgel of dried wood. He stirred around with it in the growth at his feel. And then a cry broke from his lips.

"Ach, du lieber Gott—gnädiger Gott in Himmel! Sieh' da!'

"I looked where he was pointing. His hand trembled violently—and little wonder! The stick, for about twelve inches up, was a mass of gray!

"And as I watched, I saw, steadily growing before my eyes, that awful gray creep up and surround the wood. I'm not exaggerating; in less time than it takes to tell, it had almost reached Von Housmann's hand. He threw it from him with an exclamation of horror.

"It fell into the gray growth and instantly vanished. It seemed to melt away.

"Sigmund looked at me. He was pale. At last he sighed.

"'So-o-o! Ve learn. On vood it grows. I might haf guessed. Dot iss der reason dot no trees are here. It destroys dem. But so *schnell; ach,* lige fire it growed. My friendt, I lige dot stuff lesser *als* before. It it not healt'y. But vot will it not eat?'

"I handed him my rifle. He took it, and poked the growth with the muzzle. Man, my hair fairly stood on end! Do you know anything about fungi? No? Well, I have never known or heard of any vegetable growth that would attack blue steel. But that stuff—

I tell you, that rifle barrel sprouted a crop of that gray mass as quickly as had the wood!

"I grabbed the gun and lifted it out of the patch. Already several inches of steel had been eaten—literally *eaten*—off. I held it up and watched that damnable gray crawl along the barrel. It just seemed to melt the metal. It melted like sealing-wax, and great gray flakes dropped off to the ground.

"Nearer and nearer it came—to the rear sight, the trigger-guard, the hammer. It was uncanny—like a dream. I stood there, paralyzed. I could not believe what my eyes told me was true. I looked at Sigmund. His mouth was open and his face was white as death. I laughed at his face. That seemed to tear away the mist. He yelled and pointed, and I looked down.

"Not two inches from my hand was that mass. I could see those feelers reaching out toward my hand, and I was sick. Instinctively, I threw the gun from me, aimlessly, blindly. It fell on the sand belt outside the gray mass.

"Hardly had it struck the sand before the growth had reached the butt, and then there was nothing to be seen but a tiny patch of that gray, poisonous Thing. And as we looked, it began to melt. Gradually, steadily, it was disappearing.

"'Quick, quick,' shouted Von Housmann, and we ran over to the spot. By bending over, we could see what was happening.

"The feelers, or antennae, which we had noticed before, had vanished, but instead, at the base of each individual plant, there were similar tendrils, but more of them—thousands and thousands of them all feeling and groping frantically about. And as they swayed and twisted and brushed the sand, one by one they shriveled up and seemed to withdraw into the parent body.

"Gradually this nucleus itself shrank and withered, until it was no more than a tiny gray speck on the sand. Soon that was all that was left: a lot of tiny whitish particles, much lighter in color than the original plant, scattered around on the sand.

"I looked at Von Housmann, and he looked at me. After a long interval, he spoke, slowly, almost as though it were a painful effort.

"'Ant'ony, ve haf seen a—miracle. From vot, or how, or ven, dot hell-growt' sprang, I do not know. I do not know how many, many years it has stood here; maybve it has been here for centuries. But I do know dis: if dot sand was not here—vell, I shudder to t'ink off vot would be today.'

"I stared.

"'You do not understand? *Ach, so!* You haf seen vot happened to dot stick? Und to dot gun off steel? So! Look, now.'

"He took off his hat and went over to the border of the patch. He touched—just barely touched the brim of the hat to the gray matter and held it up. Already a growth was moving up the linen. He nodded, then threw it away, onto the sand. Speechless, we watched it fade away under the merciless attack of that horrible stuff, and then, in turn, the gray fungoid growth wither and disappear.

"'Now do you understand? Do you see vot I meant? Vood, steel, linen—eferyt'ing vot it touches it *eats*. It grows fast—like flame in dry sticks—all-consuming. Aber—*siehst du?*—dot sand, ven it touched dot, it died. It starved. Und see! Look close—more closer still—at dot sand. Do you see anyt'ing odd about it?'

"I shook my head. It looked very fine and light, but I could not see anything unusual.

"'No? Iss it not glass, dot sand? Look at it under der sand vere dot T'ing has not been, and see if it is not so different.'

"I picked up some sand from under my foot. And then I saw what he had seen at once. The sand in my hand was coarser, dirtier—in short, like any fine-grained sand you may have seen. But the sand where the gray stuff had fallen was clear, glass-like. It was almost transparent, and I saw that what was there was a mass of silica particles. I nodded.

"'Yes,' I said. 'I see now. That stuff has eaten out every particle of mineral, of dirt and dust, but not the silica!'

"'Egsactly! Und dot iss vot has safed us from—Gott only knows vot! I do not know vot dot stuff vill eat, but I *do* know it vill not eat silica. Vy? I do not know. Dot is yet a mystery. So, it starts; *ach,* dot too, I do not know—but it starts somewhere. Und it eats and grows, and grows und eats, und eferyt'ing vot it touches it consumes—egsept sand. Sand stops it.

"'It eats out der stuff in der sand, but not der silica, und starves und dies. It is a miracle. If der sand vas not here—ach, Gott!—it vould keep on going until—vell, I do not know! I haf nefer seen dot before. I am intrigued, und I am going to take dot stuff—oh, only a liddle bit!—und I shall not rest until I haf learned somet'ing bout it. Und because I haf seen it does not lige sand, I vill make for it a cage—a liddle box of glass, und study it lige it vas a bug. Not?'

"We returned to where our natives still stood with our packs. We quickly fitted together some microscopic slides into a rough box and bound it about with string. With it, we returned to the edge of the gray patch. Von Housmann knelt down and carefully scooped up a bit of the fungus with a glass spatula. He dumped this into his box and waited. In five minutes it had disappeared. He look up blankly.

"'You forgot, Sigmund,' I said, smiling at his woful expression. "It starves on silica. It won't live in glass.'

"'*Ach. Dummkopf!* Of course! I haf forgot dot. But ve vill fool dot hell-plant. He goes yet on hunger-strike—no? Ve try now dot forcible feeding.'

"He took out his knife and cut several small splinters from a nearby tree.

"'Ve vill feed him, so. Dot vood, it vill be for him a great feast, und he shall eat und eat, und ve vill study him und see vot ve vill see.'

"Laughing, he bent over and shook out the tiny gray residue which was in the box. He dropped in a sliver of wood and was bending over to refill his box when I felt a sting on my foot. I looked down, and my heart stood still.

"On my shoe, just in between the laces, was a spot of gray. I could not move. I was cold. I can not describe how I felt, but I seemed turned to stone. My flesh quivered and shrank and I was sick—very sick. Sigmund looked up, startled, and then he looked at my feet.

"The next thing I knew I was on my back, my foot in his hand. One slash of his knife across the thongs which laced my boot, and he jerked it off.

"The biting grew worse. I heard him gasp, and then I felt a sharp pain. My head swam and I must have fainted. I regained consciousness—I don't know how soon after—and I found myself back under the trees. I looked at my foot, which was throbbing and burning like fire. It was swathed in a bandage that Von Housmann had taken from his emergency kit and was wrapping around the instep. It was deeply stained with blood.

"I moved, and he looked up. He smiled when he saw I was conscious.

"Dot vas a close shave—yes? It had just eaten into der shoe as I pulled it off, und one spot—like a bencil-dot—on your skin vas gray. So I cut it out and all around it, und so you haf a hole in your foot, but—you haf your foot. Now so! You lie here, und I get der niggers and ve take you to bed.'

"A tent was soon erected and I was carried into it. For two days I lay there, delirious much of the time. Sigmund never left my side. He even slept there. He was insistent that it was his fault. He said one of the apparently dead fungi had dropped on my shoe and had revived there. That is, the plant, instead of dying, had shriveled up, but the life-nucleus was still strong. I shudder even now when I think of what might have been.

"At the end of the third day I was able to hobble about a little with the aid of a cane. That afternoon Sigmund came to me and asked if I would care to go with him to fill his little glass box. I refused, and he laughed. It was the last time I ever heard him laugh. I begged him to leave that stuff alone.

"Still laughing, he made some light reply and left me. I lay in my cot. I was filled with forebodings. The heat was intense, and I must have dropped off to sleep. I dreamed horrible, troublesome, weird dreams. I awoke, bathed in a cold sweat. I felt sure that something was wrong, that someone was calling for me. I got to my feet and left my tent. No one was in sight. I tried to laugh at my premonition. I bitterly regretted that I had allowed my friend to override my persuasions.

"Hurrying as much as was possible, I started toward the clearing. My wound throbbed and ached. Once I stumbled in my eagerness. It was horrible—like a nightmare.

"I must have covered half the distance when I heard a scream. What a shriek it was! I wake up nights even now hearing it. It was unrecognizable—like some unearthly animal. Just that one scream. My stick hindered me. I threw it away and ran.

"My blood was cold in my veins, but I felt not one twinge of pain in my foot. At last I came to the edge of the clearing. And there—God, it makes me sick even now to think of it."

The speaker paused. His face was chalky, and he shuddered and buried his face in his hands. I think he was crying.

Outside, the wind still howled, dully, monotonously, eerily. Sometimes it would shriek and scream. Then my friend's voice again—level, dead, cold.

"I looked out; I saw Sigmund standing on the sand. I can see him as plainly as though he were here now. His face was ashen. He was looking down. At his feet were the fragments of the glass box he had made.

"He was holding out his hands, looking at them. They were gray. And they writhed and twisted, but his arms were still. He was not even trembling. My tongue clove to the roof of my mouth, and my throat was dry—but at last I called to him.

"'Sigmund! Sigmund!' I cried. 'For God's sake—'

"He looked up, and I tell you, I never want to see such a face again! I can never forget it. It was the face of a soul in torture. He looked at me and held out his arms. His hands were gone—flaked off in large gray, writhing drops to the sand at his feet!

"He tried to smile, but couldn't.

"Another gray blob dropped off. I was dizzy with sickness. It was unbelievable. And then he spoke. His voice was well-nigh unrecognizable. It croaked and broke:

"'Done for, my friendt. I feel it eating to my heart. Be merciful and help me. *Shoot*—quick, through der foreheadt!'"

"His words beat through the stupor clouding my brain. I started toward him, my hands outstretched. I could not speak.

"'*Um Gottes Willen, bleibt da!* Stop! Stop!'

"'Do not come near me! Vould you also be so tormented? Vot dot Gray touches it consumes. Do not argue, I say, but shoot! *Heilige Mutter!* Vy do you not shoot?'

"His voice rose into a shriek of agony. What was left of one arm had sloughed off, and the other was almost gone. A little mound of gray grew larger at his feet. His flesh was consumed, skin, blood and bone absorbed by that vile gray Thing, and he shrieked in agony and prayer. Both arms were gone, and the stuff at his feet had already begun to eat through his boots.

"I shot him, between the eyes. I saw him fall, and I fainted. When I came to, there was only a mound of tiny gray fungi, greedily reaching out their hellish tentacles for sustenance and slowly shriveling into tiny light gray specks of dust on a glossy patch of sand."

Norn

Lireve Monet

Lireve Monet

Lireve Monet was a pen-name used by Everil Worrell for this one story, which appeared in Weird Tales in February 1936. Why she chose to hide behind the pseudonym is a mystery. Eighteen stories under her own name appeared in "The Unique Magazine" from 1926 through 1954. This story is of particular interest because of the gender of the narrator. While a number of women wrote for Weird Tales, most stories were told from the male viewpoint. In "Norn," both protagonist and antagonist are women.

Norn
Lireve Monet

My first recollections of my aunt date back almost to infancy. I was passionately fond of her, so fond of her that when she was about I never cared much for my mother. I can see them both now, as they were in the early years—Mother rather tall, graciously full of figure, often laughing, a little mercurial in temper, but with the kindest, sweetest, most whimsical pair of gray eyes that ever shone beneath soft brown hair. Norn—whether the name meant what I took it from my early reading to mean: the Norse word "Fate"; or whether it was a childish contraction of some more usual name, such as "Norma", I shall never now discover. Norn, I started to say, was the name of the idolatrously worshipped aunt; and I not only loved the name as being a part of her, but also thought it highly appropriate. She was still taller than my mother, and in a different way—a rangy, long-limbed height most unusual. I have known her to boast that her arms were longer than those of any man she had ever seen, and I believe it. Her features, too, were unusual in their stern, thin-lipped, long-jawed precision, but to me they were more fascinating that any I had ever contemplated. Her eyes were coldly gray, with large, black pupils which never dilated or contracted, but were always set a certain size. As I read what I have written, my picture of Norn—I never called her Aunt—sounds strangely forbidding. I do not know if, in my childhood, I had ever shrunk from her; I know my own child did, on later coming into her presence; but if I ever did that as a child, it was long forgotten in the early mists of infantile perceptions before my acquaintance with her seems to be recorded clearly in my mind.

Beside Norn, my mother, called unusual and fascinating by many people whom we knew, faded into complete nonentity. Her very high spirits seemed trivial and foolish; I can never remember hearing Norn laugh aloud. My mother's occasional lapses from good temper seemed pointless and ineffective in contrast to the cold disapproval, or rarer cold furies, of this favorite aunt. Strange that I should have idolized her—the aunt? But I have painted only half the picture. This aunt, cold toward most of her contemporaries, knew occasional attachment to young children which amounted to a longing and craving for them—for their childish caresses, their admiration. One reason I never cared for my mother when we were with Norn was that my mother was usually busy. Norn did what work about the house she liked to do, sporadically and occasionally. She had a grim love of heavy tasks, and would do the hardest things by choice, avoiding and detesting the routine operations of cooking; and this arrangement of her occupation left her considerable time for me. She would spend hours daily, sometimes whole days at a time, holding me in a close embrace, telling me stories, reading to me, working puzzles. . . .

My mother and I are visiting on the old Iowa farm which Norn has not yet left, in one of my earliest memory-pictures. It is late afternoon of a winter day, and the bluish tinge of early dusk is creeping over the snow-fields.

"Norn! Put that child down and make her stir around a little. I want to get her out of doors before it is too late. She hasn't stuck her nose outside today—and she's sat listening to you for three hours without moving. She doesn't eat or sleep so well when she does that all day—"

"You'd better go, Mary Rose. Your mother doesn't want you to listen to me any longer."

No straight answering flare of open anger in reply to my mother's criticism; only the level look of those coldly gray eyes with the large, unchanging pupils. But I felt unutterable things: that my mother was foolishly, pettishly interfering; that, probably, she was jealous of my adoration of Norn; that she was showing an inclination to interfere with the deepest longings and yearnings of my childish nature; that I must defend myself against my mother, now and in the days to come. I looked into Norn's eyes and thought those things. Later, when it was really night and the lamplight shone in my mother's eyes as she tucked me into bed and gave me my good-night kiss, I could not quite remember those other things I had thought about her. Her eyes were gray too—a warm gray, like the soft gray blanket she still wrapped and rocked me in sometimes—"babied" me in, Norn said. My mother's baby-ing would be only for a little while at a time, bedtimes, or in little spells of illnesses, or in odd moments, but I knew that Norn thought the things my mother did with me were silly. I supposed they were. I didn't remember what Mother had done this after-noon—she had been unreasonable, mean, to me and Norn when we were happy together. But of course, Mother was—Mother. . . .

My eyes were shutting, and as I fell asleep I was wrapped around in the warm gray light that was so different from that other. Little children are so much younger, just at bedtime.

Father and Mother never got along very well, and I thought in my baby-days that was Father's fault. He was very wise and clever; I often heard him sneering at the minds of other people, though never at Norn's mind. He sneered at Mother, though, very openly. He had married mentally beneath him, and some money both he and Mother had expected her to inherit had been left in the wrong place, and that had gone against Father's plans. I knew without being told that each of them wished they had not married, but that my mother's whole life was bound up in me, while Father had not that compensation. Men are different. Norn helped to teach me that men are on a bigger plane, and children are to admire and revere their fathers very much whether they feel that they know them very well or not, and whether or not their fathers seem to care very much about them. Also, if men are disagreeable around home, it is the responsibility of the wife and mother to make them feel agreeable. A successful wife always does that, but my mother never managed it.

With my eleventh year came a parting which agonized me. The Iowa farm was sold. My father, whose business had been in a small, Middle Western town, moved east. Norn came with us to visit, as did also another aunt, Mugsie, a fattish indeterminate sort of aunt, with her little girl Dorothy, a blonde, plump, babyish thing like her mother and yet unlike her, since Dottie was utterly and ir-resistibly adorable. I shall never forget the utter sweetness, the innocence of Dottie's clear blue eyes, or the warmth of her baby smile. I loved her with all my little-girl heart, and longed for her back as I longed for Norn. I was to have them again. . . .

●   ●   ●

Norn decided to go to the west coast with Aunt Mugsie and
Dottie, who were shortly to join Dottie's father there. I listened to
my mother talking this over with Norn. Though I think she must
have been jealous of Norn's domination of me, of her assumption
of superiority, and of the superiority conceded to her by every
member of the family, my mother joined in the universal admiration—which amounted nearly to adoration—of Norn.

"Stay with us, Norn. You and Mugsie will have a good time,
but after all, Mugsie can't get around and keep up with you. You
and I would go to shows, camp in summer—we're both so much
more energetic. And I've always looked after you, made your
clothes and fixed them, because I was the oldest girl—you'll miss
that."

"Mugsie will learn to do those things for me." There wasn't an
idea that Norn would wait on herself.

"Mugsie *is* selfish. She barely looks after herself."

Norn fixed my mother with that gray gaze.

"I say Mugsie will learn to look after me. Besides, Mugsie and
Ralph are going to have money. I think Ralph's investments on the
coast will be very good, very soon. I can use a lot of money, and
money comes where money is. I care a good deal about having
the things I want. I know exactly what I want, and I am going with
Mugsie."

That ended that talk, but there was another. I don't know
where Norn met Mr. Wolf. I didn't know—I never learned, and
can't conjecture now, the nationality of Mr. Wolf. He was the head
of a sports-goods establishment, and he employed mostly foreign-
ers—Jews, Armenians, a Chinaman of the tall, raw-boned Chu Chin
Chow type. I have heard Mr. Wolf accused of being all those vari-
ous things—Jewish, Armenian, Chinese or Tartar, and I have seen
him smile suavely and answer "No." The name, of course, is English, but the word "wolf" is known to every race. I am sure the
Jews and Armenians in his store feared him. I was never so sure
about the Chinaman, but then I have never had to do with Orien-
tals.

Norn brought Mr. Wolf to the house one evening, and it developed that by an odd chance he was going to establish a large
branch of his business in the coast city to which Norn was going
with Mugsie, and that Norn was to be his secretary-treasurer.

"But that's almost the whole executive staff, and Norn has only studied a little shorthand!" my mother cried in amazement which held an undertone of sheer consternation. "I never heard of—"

That suave smile of Mr. Wolf's bared his gleaming teeth for the first time in my presence, as he laid a hand ever so lightly, yet ever so possessively, on Norn's arm.

"A marvelous intellect—a genius for efficiency!" he said, and I believed him—yet wondering how he could know so soon. And then that thought faded before other thoughts.

He was like Norn! Norn was a good six feet tall, and slender, yet showing, somehow, steel-like strength in every fiber; long-limbed and rangy; awkward with her feet and hands, I know now, though my childish idolatry did not permit that observation then; awkward of foot and hand and wrist and ankle, as though those hands were made for no ordinary tasks, in their long-boned strength, as though the shoes she wore never quite did justice to the freedom of the stride which ought to be hers. And Mr. Wolf was like that too, well over six feet, and thin with a steel-like, rangy strength. His jaws and facial bones were long and clearly cut, and his hands and feet seemed somehow a little out of the picture, a little out of place—no such thought of Norn's feet and hands had entered my mind then; but even then I noticed that characteristic of Norn's voice, very low and husky for a woman's, which I found in his voice also, and because I loved the sound of Norn's voice I conceded tht Mr. Wolf's voice was beautiful. And there was a likeness in their eyes—a steady coldness of gaze, a likeness of pupil—Mr. Wolf's eyes were a lightish amber-brown, but the pupils, like Norn's, were enormous, and did not change or alter in the slightest degree.

It was a partnership that was to last and be life-long, and though I saw that similarity, and though I admired Mr. Wolf, I hated the thought of it then. And when they all went west together, driving in Mr. Wolf's low-hung, gray car, I cried days and nights until my eyes were swollen day-long and my pillow wet night-long, and I could eat nothing Mother fixed for me.

She cured me—Mother—by giving me a kitten, after the storm had spent itself. I felt it was silly of me to be so won by a ball of gray and white fluff, to learn laughter again from the kitten's crazy antics. But I was only eleven, and little girls whose hearts have been broken are so babyish, so peculiarly their mother's again, for just a little while.

A year later we visited the west coast. That visit was the first real horror of my life.

Norn resented our coming, or rather she resented my mother's presence. She would have been glad to have me, but she did not want her. I wondered what was so wrong with my mother, why she was so unwelcome. I looked down on her for not being desirable in Norn's eyes. The old fascination had reasserted itself in me with terrific strength. I was eleven now, nearly twelve; and people said that I was a very beautiful young girl. I had hair darker than Mother's, which curled naturally, and black-lashed dark eyes which I knew held a good deal of expression and appeal. Strangers talked about my coloring and said that I was like the second part of my name, Mary Rose. I would look in the glass and wonder what it was that made them notice me. I looked so ordinary beside Norn, who was wearing expensive clothes now that made her appear very distinguished and exotic, besides being exquisitely groomed. In my adolescent acuteness of perception I noticed for the first time that queer awkwardness of hand and foot which she could not overcome; but it drew me to her, that one so over-whelming should condescend to a human imperfection, as I thought of it. I noticed, too, rather in spite of myself, a something raucous in the husky voice, and though my ears were very sensi-tive, I grew used to that again, as I had been used to it in my child-hood. I saw the coldness and hardness in the fixed, gray gaze more clearly, and that did fascinate and draw me with all the greater power—because those great gray eyes glowed on my face with a yearning, possessive sort of hunger, when we sat and talked alone in the twilight. (Norn hated lights, and would never have turned on a light in evening or dark night if she had lived by her-self.)

Afterward, Norn said that everything was my mother's fault, and my mother, who turned against Norn at last, said that every-thing was Norn's fault. There was a terrific fight one morning, over some trivial domestic detail. It was a holiday, and on holidays Norn always gave everybody directions as to just what they were to do. I know that at first I thought it was about nothing, and suddenly voices rose and rose, till I could hardly tell what they were talking about, but Norn was—actually—ordering my mother to leave, to get out of the house, telling her she was not wanted there. My mother seemed to be reproaching Norn with memories of the old days when she had rather mothered her—but Norn said Mother was getting personal and not telling the truth, and that she was a liar. Then Mother called Norn a liar, and suddenly Norn seemed to leap out of herself. I can think of no other phrase.

She seemed to lengthen out, to tower even taller, to grow beyond the natural size of any woman. She did leap forward, but it was something more than that. It was like the unleashing of a thing in prison. It was a cold, violent, elemental fury that was not like any anger I had ever seen. It was more like—far more like— the dart of a lightning-bolt out of a storm-racked sky.

It seemed to me that she struck Mother in the face, and that Mother struck blindly, without hitting Norn at all. It seemed that Norn knocked her down, or threw her to the floor, that she was actually hanging over her, crouching down in a posture not like that I had ever seen a human being assume. . . .

There was a shifting and a changing. Was it the actual picture in that room, or in my swimming sense-perceptions, or in my mind itself? Certainly the room had changed—other people had come into it. Mugsie and Ralph, little Dottie—my Uncle Robert, who had turned up in town a few days before.

Norn was standing erect now, her thin, finely chiseled lips drawn back over her rather large, even white teeth, her breath coming hard, her eyes for once seeming dilated beyond their wont. And my mother was lying in a crumpled heap on the floor, sobbing—and she was too large a woman to lie in a crumpled heap, and, after one look in Norn's eyes, I was ashamed of my mother.

"You all saw! I never lose control of myself. My nerves are iron. I had nothing to do with this. She flew at me and I pushed her away, and she threw herself down there, as no decent woman would, in a neurotic tantrum. No one can have any respect for her, after this, in this whole family."

I was watching Norn as she turned that steady, cold gaze into the eyes of each person in the room in turn—she had looked into my eyes first of all. She looked last at little Dot. And I was more ashamed of my mother than ever, as she scrambled awkwardly to her feet, the very personification of futile, embarrassed, outraged and uncomprehending rage. I saw them all, as they looked back at Norn. It reminded me of stories of mediaeval days, when allegiance was sworn to some mighty queen without the need of a spoken word.

My mother and I returned to the East and to my father, and soon after that we bought the home that was ours through the years of my growing up. This was a darling little house with a shingled top which stood on a hill surrounded by beautiful trees, and which seemed deeply endeared to my spirit from the first day they brought me to see it. We were all three happy there in spite of the fact that sentiment had long since died between my mother and father. Young as I was, I felt the coming of a greater peace into our home after the pretenses and demands of their youth had definitely failed between them. Those two were mismated, but there was something essentially sound in those days in my father's nature, and there was an infinity of sweetness and fineness in Mother, and with greater maturity the two of them achieved, with me, a lovely home. I remember yet how happily the flames seemed to play in the wide brick fireplace, as though they were a sort of bright and shining genius of the place.

And I remember how sweetly and naturally, here, my nature blossomed into love.

Kerry Shane was the fulfilment of life, to me, and I married him, in my early twenties, and went away with him—with frequent visits home during the five years of our life together. When he died suddenly, of a cramp taken while swimming in the surf of the south Long Island shore, I took our baby and went home to live. My baby was a girl, named after me—Mary Rose. Kerry had called me Rose, without the Mary, and sometimes it was Rosebud. He said I reminded him always of very young, of incurably young things, like a rosebud or the crescent moon. Not that that has anything to do with my story, which is more the story of Norn, and not that kind of thing.

Mother had been all broken up over my marriage, which had taken the center out of the home she had finally welded so finely together. Now she was broken by Kerry's death, in feeling that the whole thing—my marriage—had been futile—agonizing to her, and ending in heartbreak for me. She resented my grief, which I could not altogether conceal, wanting me back in my old, untouched girlhood. She turned to little Mary Rose in passionate devotion, but she was never quite herself, it seemed to me, and six months after Kerry's death she died too, of a cold which had seemed very trivial.

As for me, I had, long before her passing, achieved a considerable degree of contentment, except for worrying about her. Kerry, it seemed to me, was not so very far away from me. I seemed to see rifts of light in the heavy curtain men call death—these are things impossible to explain, but very real to me. I still loved the house on the hill, set around by fine tree. And I idolized, worshipped and adored little Mary Rose, who looked at me out of eyes that were mine—and his—thus eternally united. I could picture a long life of happy usefulness, nurturing, guiding, launching and always loving little Mary Rose.

I shall never forget the night Dan Reavers called with a woman he said he wanted me to meet.

"This is an incomparable honor for you, Mary Rose," Dan said to me. "Mrs. McDonald never goes out to people's homes professionally. They come to her and pay well enough for that. She likes me—I don't know why.

"I told her about you—about your bereavement, Mary. I thought—perhaps I thought she'd have a message from Kerry, though she never knows whether she will or not, or just what she will get. Anyhow—something seemed to be driving me, fairly, to see that you two met—and here in your home."

At Mrs. McDonald's suggestion we sat silently for a while, in a darkened room, my father being away. And she did speak of Kerry, dreamily, giving me several messages that surprized me, rather.

But what she said of Kerry was only in line with thoughts that seemed to come to me directly from him—to stream in upon my life as the light of the suns streams into a darkened corner. And again, it has little or nothing to do with my story. It has to do with my story, that, suddenly, she spoke of the house.

"This house. Mrs. Shane, I wish you could leave it. There are places that are said to have a *genius loci*. That means, there is a spirit of the place, usually benevolent, sometimes not; and if it is evil, it is hard to prevail against it—to be good or happy there, or even—safe."

She paused. I burst impetuously into speech. I loved our old house!

"This house is not like that, Mrs. McDonald. We've been—in spite of the things life brings—we've been happy here."

"I know that, child. But this house is not the kind of place I just described, but its direct opposite. There is another kind of place which is a sort of focusing-point for whatever enters there. You and all of yours have been, in varying degrees, spirits of the light. Good, and not evil souls have crossed this threshold, and it has, when life's normal rhythm flowed through its walls, heightened the brightness of its current.

"But the people who have dwelt here are ordinary people— you, Mrs. Shane, very psychic, but with undeveloped powers; your mother, your husband, bright spirits a little psychic too—not quite so much. Your baby—only a baby as yet. Your father—there's something undefined. . . .

"Something else is coming into this place. I feel the creeping of a long, cold shadow. Something dark. Something cruel. A sinister thing. Can't you stop it, Mrs. Shane? Do you know what— whom—I mean?

"No." She answered herself. "You'll know soon, but you won't be able to stop it. Paths cross where they are fore-ordained to cross. Too much love is a challenge to the powers of darkness, Mary Rose—and there has been much love in your life. Your husband loved you as few women are loved—and still loves, across the narrow Border. Still his love reaches you. Your baby adores you, and your poor mother loved you too much for this world. You will understand what I say better than I can—know."

Her breathing was growing irregular. I thought, with a little fear, that she might be about to go into a trance. But she seemed to will herself out of that, and continued more steadily.

"Get away if you can, Mrs. Shane. If you can't—for money reasons, for instance—be warned, and always ready to leave. Someone is coming who has dark powers, and this place will reflect those powers, concentrate and magnify them like a burning-glass. It is a focal point, and will develop what is latent, make a true adept of one who is maliciously uncertain and stumbling. Someone is coming, and you will know who. At least, it is better to be warned."

My mother had been dead only six weeks, then, but it was on the next day that Father told me he was going to marry Norn. I did not at once think of, or remember, the evening before, or Mrs. McDonald, but I know that his words shocked me—startled, even frightened me. And that is odd, because I had long ago put down that scene between Mother and Norn as being Mother's fault. People didn't knock people down, leap at them, crouch over them. Norn had let me see, before we left, that she still loved me. She had wanted me. She had told me I would be happier with her, asked me to ask my mother to give me to her. We had had whispered talks, huddling together in the dusk, before I went away with Mother out of that keen sense of duty a child so often knows, and is so seldom credited with having.

I ought to have said, too, that in keeping with the great vein of generosity she had often manifested—or perhaps partly because, as she scrambled ignominiously from the floor at Norn's feet that day long ago, Mother too had looked deeply into her eyes— Mother had let me visit Norn. Always and always the old domination had reasserted itself. I was a child worshipping at a shrine…

And now I know that is the reason for the sick shrinking of my heart at my father's words.

I had been a child, worshipping at a shrine; but I was no child now. I was a woman—baptized to womanhood by love, and by the birth of a child, and by bereavement. Perhaps it took all of those three to weld my soul to what it was now—a thing that stood alone, fairly its own creature, and looked back at the Norn of my childhood with the eyes of a woman. She could not, again, dominate me—not even so much as she had dominated my mother. I did not want her to dominate my baby. And I remembered that she had always disliked or scorned women—reduced them to a sort of slavery, as she did with Mugsie, or hated them as she had Mother. She would hate me, and I would still be myself, owning and knowing incurably my unchangeable self and soul, refusing to be swallowed up and diminished to nothing. And she would be

my stepmother, and—all at once I knew this—the thing that was
really wrong with Father was, you couldn't trust him. He could be
made into almost anything, but not by a daughter. It would take
woman's hands, *his woman's hands,* and not hands like my
mother's that had not cared either to mold or to caress him. Norn,
though—she could mold him into any shape. Yes, into any shape.

I shuddered in the June air. And it was only after that, that I
remembered Mrs. McDonald's words last night.   I had been
shocked out of rememberance of lesser things.

One midsummer day Norn came to our house on the hill.
Father had met her in a strange city half-way between the coasts,
and now he brought her home. It was an hour of golden twilight
when they came up to the porch. Mary Rose—brown curls all over
her head, running and talking and a perfect darling nearly two
years old now—was crawling in a last shaft of sunlight. And suddenly that ray of light faded, and it was dark. Clouds coming up in
the west? Oh, yes, of course, it was perfectly natural, but I say that
our place was altered in that moment. The tall trees told secrets
that they had not known a moment before. All their whispering
had been kindly, and they had stood like guardians around the
hosue. They were guardians no longer. Aloof, stern, ready—*hoping*—to look on tragedy. What tragedy, I wondered? And my
heart whispered: "Something is going to happen here."

At the steps, Norn paused and looked deep into my eyes. She
had aged—and developed. Truly, there was something timelessly
unchanging about the tall, thin woman standing there in the dusk.
Her eyes gleamed, and her teeth—she had perfect teeth, I saw.
The lines of her mouth were set and firm as of old—but had they
been so cruel?

Her eyes held mine, compelling me to a reply. And I gave the
reply in spite of myself. I wanted to fool her, to play for time. I
wanted to rear little Mary Rose nicely, not to skimp on her food
and clothes and doctor's bills and future education—those things,
living on in this house would mean to me. Could I do it? I could
try, and I wanted to veil my eyes from Norn. But my eyes were
always true mirrors of my thoughts, I know; and they were then.
In her eyes I saw the knowledge grow—the knowledge that she
could bully, but not dominate; frighten, but not absorb; dictate

without conquering. All I wanted in the whole, wide world was fredom of soul, and a safe and happy future for little Mary Rose. Norm wanted—what darkly, deeply schemed, strange things? Complete dominion of my father's every thought, she wanted. And that she would have. She wanted more. . . .

Her eyes left mine, furious in defeat, and turned upon my child. And little Mary Rose cringed back, trembling, and ran to me and clung to me.

"You haven't taught her very pleasant manners!" Norn said abruptly, and passed on into the house. My father lingered behind her.

"If you can't get that child to behave respectfully and politely, you'll have to begin to spank her. Spanking doesn't hurt—"

"I do spank her. I spank her hard when she does things that will hurt her. I spanked her three times for turning on the gas heater. She's a little too young to make pretend to like people—"

"She's not too young to learn manners!"

It was the first of my bitter arguments—bad for me, and bad for Mary Rose, the child. But within a month Norn had won so much of Mary Rose's heart that I trembled. And my trembling was not jealousy. I was afraid of Norn, in a queer, wordless way. . . .

June passed and July came, and it was a hot July; a month of drought.

And near the end of that month we had company. Mr. Wolf, like Norn unchanged, except to be older and harder-looking, driving a still longer, lower-hung, gay car, and bringing with him Norn's favorite niece with whom she had lived out these long years—little Dottie. Little Dottie no more, as I remembered her, but changed—so strangely. Not intensified, but altered. Sly, where she had been candid. Something almost rodent in her blonde, red-lipped face under the perfect blonde marcel. To look at her made me feel sick, remembering the child she had been; made me brood by little Mary Rose when she was asleep, longing to keep her close, to hold her spirit close to my spirit. For Dorothy now was a shell of something left tenantless, and operated by something alien from without—or so it seemed to me.

About this time we all went to see *Rasputin and the Empress*. And I think the picture precipitated things for us. To me it was so horrible—the sinister altering and absorbing of the innocent child-spirit of the young prince by the hypnotic powers of Rasputin. I was looking for jobs, for apartments, furnished rooms—and a telephone call came for me from one of the men I had inteviewed about a position, and the message came into Norn's hands.

When she gave it to me, I knew that it was the beginning of the end of some pretense that had been between us. And I wanted to move that very day, but waited. Positions that paid anything at all were almost non-existent, and I was still hoping for something better than I had found.

Night came, and it was the night of the full moon. In the room I shared with little Mary Rose, the air was motionless, and almost too hot to breathe. Outside the windows, the black leaves hung on the boughs of the trees, motionless. Those trees seemed weighted down with doom, hushed, expectant.

Mary Rose was restless in her sleep that night, and a beam from the moon kept reaching her face, her closed eyelids. I moved and shifted her bed, but I could not push it far from the window on so hot a night. I thought the direct moonlight bad for her, and perhaps making her moan and toss. But there was nothing I could do about it, and at last I fell into an exhausted sleep.

It was midnight by my watch when I woke suddenly. I glanced, instantly and instinctively, as every mother does, at my child. And her bed was empty.

My heart thudded heavily, sick with terror. Mad fears of kidnappers hurtled dizzily into my mind. I ran, heavily, like a person in a nightmare, into the hall. And then I saw my little Mary Rose.

There was a window in the curve of the stairway, and the moon shone in there on her, as she made her way—slowly and falteringly—down the stairs. I called to her:

"Mary Rose! Rose! You're sleep-walking. Don't fall."

I had made my voice very soft, as I hurried to her.

"I'll take you back to bed. Into Mother's bed. We'll cuddle, till you go sound back to sleep. Mother will pin you in so you don't get away again."

I shall never forget the face she turned on me in the moonlight—and she was not two! There was something in that little baby face that was utterly an anachronism. It was not merely hate, though that was there too. It was a sense of outrage—as though I were a stranger, say, tearing her from her mother's arms, and pre-

tending to be her mother. I have imagined that, of course. I do
not know whether it would be possible for any child to look again
as I saw my own child look that night. I know that I got clearly the
message of her baby mind, which was that she was through with
me (at less than two years old!); that she was going—God knew
where—to do her own little will—God knew what!

It made me sick, as the thought of kidnappers had made me
sick. But I was her mother, of course, and I did not falter. I knew
there was something here that I must get at the roots of. To have
caught her in my arms, dragged her to our room, spanked her into
submission, pinned her into bed—this would all have been possible. I did not think it the thing to do.

"You'll have to tell me where you want to go, Mary Rose." I
kept my voice steady, but defiance shrilled in her baby voice.

"To Norn. I want to go with Norn."

"Go where?"

Slyness. On a baby face. That was another thing I had never
seen.

"Maybe nowhere, Muvver. Maybe to sleep with her. I want
Norn. Then, when she does go somewhere, I want to go too."

"But is she going somewhere?"

"I don't know. Oh, no, no, no!" (An old baby phrase of impatience.) "Norn told me I could come to her any time. This
Norn's house. She said so. Norn! Norn!"

My aunt came hurrying out of the room she shared with my
father.

"I think you're demented, Mary." (We had all rather dropped
the lat part of my name, leaving it for my baby; and Mary always
meant me.) "I think you're utterly insane. You mistreat this child
horribly. She should be taken from you. Some day, I'll see you
can't torment her any more. You're insanely jealous, a cruel
mother. She wants to come to me in the middle of the night—and
no doubt you know better than I, what you did to her to make her
run away from you. Children don't do such things without reason.
She wants to sleep with me anyway. She has said so. Well, I'm
taking her over tonight. I'm her best friend, and she knows it. Go
back to your room, Mary, and let the child alone. You'll sleep
without her now—"

My nerves broke.

"I will not! I'll keep her, Norn! She's my baby—you can't do
this—"

My father came out of the dark doorway of their room, rotund in his pajamas.

"I've been listening to this! You'll sleep where and how you're told to, in this house. If you want to go on seeing that child, you behave yourself. I'll support Norn's statement. No child runs crying from her mother in the dead of night without reason. You're a trouble-maker. Norn and I bear witness for each other in everything—"

Was there a mad glitter in his eyes? So rapt, so obedient to her will, yet so violating the fatherhood that must lie dormant in his breast. Yes, he could be made into—anything. Norn could do it...

The best thing to do—the best thing to do. They were on the verge of taking Mary Rose right out of my hands. Then if I planned to go away, even a day later, it might be too late. They would stand together on any story—railroad me into an asylum? That, I knew, was the backlog of their thoughts; and I remember hearing Norn tell outsiders, calmly and regretfully, that Mary Rose was not the same since her double bereavement. I wasn't insane. I'd welcome alienists—then I shuddered. Suppose they got me separated from Mary Rose, got her utterly alienated—and that she was already was. I had stood a good deal. How much more could I stand? I had studied psychology in college. I remembered the simile of the weak cart and the shallow mudhole. Well, my mental cart was stout enough, and proven over and over; but this hole was pretty deep—deep as they could make it. . . .

God! How little I knew that they could dig a pit under my very feet, which would be bottomless, a slimy gateway to the depths of hell!

So quickly it happened. There are not words for the lightning speed of the next moments. . . .

As though aroused by our commotion, two others appeared with silent swiftness. Mr. Wolf and Dorothy, from their respective rooms in the other wing of the house. And they all drew together, facing me. All together against me. All staring at me. And none of them looking—quite right—quite natural. . . .

My baby Mary Rose was clinging to Norn's hands. Her baby face was upturned, worshipfully, to that dark, long-jawed, sharply cut countenance. Before my eyes, Norn stooped to the baby and kissed her. Such a kiss! Never on this earth, I hope, has woman kissed child like that. Something was being given and taken—and the upturned baby face seemed to swim in a veritable swoon of rapturous response. I could have fainted where I stood, but my shrinking gaze, which I could no longer bear to keep upon my child, dimly comprehended the look on Dorothy's face. Dorothy hated little Mary Rose for that caress. Dorothy would like to kill Mary Rose. . . .

Mr. Wolf's eyes were on Dorothy. He would do anything she liked. His moment was to come... And did I say they all looked— *unnatural?* It was like the old nursery tale. "But, grandmother, how long your teeth are! 'The better—'"

I remembered a very horrible murder story I had read, which was based on psychological workings out of old nursery rimes. And I remembered something else.

My adult reading had carried me far into the field of ancient superstitions. Now my reason seemed toppling, as the possible reality of some of these swept into my reluctant mind. Lycanthropy—wasn't it—where certain Things could be in turn human in form and animal—and bore always the stamp of some ferocious monster traits of nature? Lycanthropy—that was it!

And as I watched those awful changes—the dizzy swimming of the air between us, through which I yet saw clearly the fast-changing, definite outlines—Norn, growing in stature, assuming a leaping posture—her face reaching out before her, the long jaw still elongating, the fixed pale glare of her wide eyes with the unchanging pupils now seeming to come to life, to shoot red sparks. . . . The long arms hanging down, now, before her—those strangely awkward feet and hands seeming at last at ease, wildly graceful, *the hands turning to wolf's paws.* . . .

Mr. Wolf, changing similarly, instant by instant. Dorothy—no, she was not a wolf. She was a sly little fox, and had dropped to all fours.

My frantic gaze sought my father's face. Not he, not he!

No. He was what he had been. A man, angry, opinionated, rotund. His easily led nature too flaccid, too plastic, perhaps, to take on any horrific alteration. But he would not, even now, sustain or support my cause. He had done what they would have wanted him to do, what they had doubtless imposed upon his subconscious mind to do. He had simply fallen asleep. My single frenzied scream did not reach his ears. He was leaning in the angle of the balustrade—and as I looked, he slipped quite simply and easily to the floor. And it came to me, that if these devils did not tear me to pieces, they could do a worse thing—they could reassume human form at will, I was sure, as I was sure that many times before they had gone into these more elemental expressions of their natures. And they could laugh at me, and sneer at me, and know that my first desperate outcry against them, my first accusation of their being the things they were, would put me for ever behind the bars. Away from little Mary Rose!

And now I was plunged into the ultima thule of horror.

Here and there the moon shone in through the windows of the dark lower story rooms, and from polished floor and furniture and light walls and ceilings a dim diffusion of its light made barely visible the gaunt form which hurled itself furiously down upon me. It was that one of the transfigured three which had worn Norn's features, which still showed a dim likeness to her: the smaller of the two monster wolf-things. And in my nightmare shock I was overtaken and overwhelmed by its first lunge. I fought my way backward, falling, falling. . . .

And how can I describe the uncanny dreadfulness of what I must try to make clear? The change from woman to wolf was yet only partial. Something was lacking—later I knew what it was that was still required to make the woman all wolf, till the rising beams of tomorrow's sun should restore the more common and original form. At any rate, it was the more concrete, physical manifestation which was not yet altered to the semblance of the beast, and to this I owe my life. Over me, muzzle near my face, eyes gleaming red in the dusky gloom, bent the wolf-head. I saw the claws that tore at my face and body—but what I felt was the large, bony hands of a woman, tearing and clawing as the claws of the beast should have done, but so much more ineffectually that I was not mangled, as the evidence of my sense of sight told my frantic brain from second to second I was about to be mangled.

Those claws tore at my face, and I felt scratches; but only the scratches of fingernails. Bony fingers closed around my left eyeball in its socket, as though they would tear it from its place. It was the sort of attack which could only be made by human hands and fingers prompted by the workings of a mind gone down to the level of a beast. Then, just as I uttered a despairing cry at the sharpness of the pain shooting from the back of my eyeball to the top and back of my head, the grip shifted, and brutish hands, that still were only hands, tore at my breast, and beat and tore and mauled at my body. I screamed out loud, and a tiny form was upon me—my little girl, rushing to my defense in spite of the spell that was upon her. The hands loosed their hold, and I staggered to my feet, circled, crouched low, got away—and dashed through the rooms of the dark and silent house.

A tiny white form leaped away before me—little Mary Rose, running madly I suppose, wild with terror, from all of us now. And I followed, with the sound of running feet behind me. And as the pack crossed a broad band of moonlight on the black floor, the sound of those following footsteps changed—awfully. It was now the clatter of claws that sounded on the polished floor, and to be overtaken by them now meant instant death.

In the kitchen I snatched from a table a sharp-bladed paring-knife that lay in a shaft of moonlight. And I half fell over something wet and slippery, as the arc made by my hand knocked down something else from the table that broke at my feet, spilling liquid.

What happened now was more horrible to me than all that had gone before. The little white figure of the flying child uttered a queer, choking cry, and rushed for the spot where the gurgle and splash had been. I saw her, prostrate on the floor, sensed that the little face went down, heard the sucking of eager little lips—

And heard another most unchildish cry, as the little thing got to her feet again. Those following monsters had paused as I paused, no doubt in exultation. Now we all flew forward again, the child ahead, I trying to overtake her and to escape myself. . . .

We circled once more through the silent house and flew out over the doorsill, and I felt the hot breath of one of the following monsters.

And as the clear light of the full moon touched my child, she dropped to all fours—a tiny, perfect wolf-cub. Straight for the forest that lay the length of a city block away, she sped. And I knew with a terrible sense of loss like the sense of loss I had felt at Kerry's death—that she would never come back to me. As she ran with the swift patter of tiny claws on the hard path, I could hear her whimpering. And yet she ran straight and fast—faster than I could go. My heart labored desperately. I had read of these dreadful transmutations. At dawn those other monsters would resume human form. They would, if by chance I had escaped death from them, love the game of baiting me to madness that they would carry on. They might even spare me for the sake of that game, if their brute fury left them reason after a while. They would love the conflict of wits, the utter deceitfulness of it, as all things evil love darkness and guile.

But little Mary Rose with the dawn would be an outcast. She would know instinctively that she had crossed a dark threshold. She would still run from me, hide from me. With what seemed like a clear vision, I actually seemed to see what would happen when dawn came to her in the little wood to which she was running for sanctuary. There was a narrow, rather deep, very muddy little stream in that wood. I could see a little body floating, a little upturned face for ever quiet. . . .

And I ran faster.

The scratch and thud of heavy, shaggy forms rising and falling on rough padded paws and scraping claws came nearer. I could feel a fetid breath fanning my shoulder. I knew the foretaste of death.

And a small, yellow body flashed by me, and I heard snarls of rage, and the pack swept by me, one huge body knocking me from my feet. Even as I scrambled up, I sensed that the immediate interest of the brutes, more imperative even than the destruction of me, their enemy, was the flying little cub ahead. And I knew a flash of sheer telepathy such as most of us have experienced in moments of desperate stress, in dealing with our kind. These were not my kind—but their instincts were primal in their force, and I felt their impact.

I had known that Dorothy hated little Mary Rose, because she was jealous of Norn's love for her. And I had known that Mr. Wolf had turned from Norn to the blonde young girl Dorothy. And now the yellow fox wanted to kill the little cub, and the largest wolf was ready to help. But the other wolf actually loved the little cub, would fight for its life, that she might make her into the unholy thing she herself had become, that she might know her comradeship in evil adventures. . . .

The yellow fox was closing in on the cub, and the huge timber wolf was ahead. Desperately I felt the knife in my hand, and raised my arm. And I seemed to hear Kerry's voice. It may, of course, have been the projection of my own sound instinct, a hallucination founded on reason. I do not know. But what I seemed to hear him say, was this:

"If you throw the knife at the wolf or the fox, you will kill whichever one you aim at, for this night your aim is as true as your need is desperate. Don't—don't! Morning will make the dead body back into the human shape it must wear by day, and you will be accused by the others. And the little cub will get away.

"Throw at the cub! Hold the knife by the blade, and throw handle first. It is the only way!"

I obeyed—as I should have obeyed if Kerry had stood at my side—as perhaps he did stand there. I shall never know that—but I obeyed what seemed to come to me clothed in his words, uttered by his voice. And my aim was true, and the little cub gave a little moan, and dropped upon the path.

The yellow fox leaped at it, and the huge wolf closed in to help the fox. But the other wolf uttered a cry that was strangely human, after all, and closed with the larger wolf, and they fought and tore each other there in the moonlight, till drops of blood flew through the air and splashed warm on my face and bare arms.

The yellow fox must have been hurt in the mêlée, for it gave a cry of pain and bounded away, toward the forest. And I came to as the blood touched my shrinking flesh—for it was like the touch of something unspeakably unclean. I crept to where the little cub was lying, for the smaller wolf, fighting desperately for her life, had forced the battle a little away from it. And did I catch the gleam from those mad, beast's eyes, of a brief, but piteous entreaty? I thought I did. But I forgot everything but the little cub as I reached it, and gathered it in my arms.

It was stunned, but I could see that it breathed, and I uttered a prayer of thankfulness. I ran back toward the house through the moonlight, hearing that awful clamor behind me, feeling death in the air. At least we were safe while the brutes fought. At the house I could lock myself in till morning. With morning, there would be only human things to contend with, and later I must get away.

I felt my eyes swimming with hot tears. The sight of that grotesque little head lying on my arm. The wolf-head—of my child. Dawnlight! Did it always bring the metamorphosis? I was not sure.

•   •   •

I reached the house and crept up the stairs. On the landing my father still slept, unless he had died in that heavy stupor. I did not pause, but gained my own room and laid my burden down on my own bed and knelt beside it. And through the night I prayed, and with the dawn it came—the heavenly change of the beast back to the likeness and being of the child I loved!

I went out of our room then, carrying her in my arms, and she nestled to me as though she knew how nearly we had been parted for ever.

In the lower hall I met my father, worried, querulous, old-looking the the dawnlight.

"I've looked for Norn everywhere. I can't find her. Last night you were quarreling with her—we'll have no more that, in this house!" he said. "She'll take over the care of the little girl. She is so wise, so efficient. You're always upset, you know. Norn has warned me that she believes you are going to get to the point of actually seeing hallucinations. You will have to be looked after, but we won't have you looking after your baby any more. But where—where is Norn?"

"When you fell asleep—" I began.

"I fainted," he corrected me irritably. "Your quarreling with Norn was too much for me. Don't do it again."

"I won't!" I promised light-heartedly. I was becoming increasingly sure that Norn would never return. Something about the house told me so—my own house again, protecting and sheltering me and my child. The very look of the morning sunlight, the sound of the birds in the tall, whispering trees, were telling me good tidings. I felt sure the monsters would never come back—would never come back. I felt sure. . . .

"After you became entirely unconscious, Mr. Wolf, Dorothy and Norn all went outside—I suppose they wanted to look at the moon. It was beautiful last night.

"Little Mary Rose ran out too, and was running away, and we all went after her. But Norn, Dorothy and Mr. Wolf got into an argument. Dorothy slipped off somewhere by herself—but I left Norn and Mr. Wolf fighting it out, down the path toward the wood. I caught up with Mary Rose and brought her back. I left them fighting—"

My father made one more effort at command.

"Don't say 'fighting'. Show some respect. Mr. Wolf has been Norn's good and lifelong friend, and if they had a disagreement—"

"They had!" I interrupted blithely. "Somehow, I believe you'll hae a chance to know where they went if you'll walk down the wood path. Please do. I will get breakfast."

He went away grumbling, and I set the table—for three. But only little Mary rose and I could eat. It was horrible, what my father found down there, and the events of the next few days were sad and gruesome. But I could not be sorry, and they did not take my appetite away. I had been through too much for that.

He found my aunt and her old friend, Mr. Wolf, literally torn to pieces beside the wood path. Some huge animals, escaped from God knew where—there was never a theory advanced to account for the marks on their bodies.

And the little yellow fox never was seen again, nor was my cousin Dorothy. Police searched for months for the yellow-haired girl, and Aunt Mugsie still writes to me sorrowfully about her. I am sorry, desperately sorry for Aunt Mugsie. Even to think of losing a child of one's own—

I know that I ought to close this record with a word of explanation; not to explain away what actually happened—not to throw up a smoke screen, to pretend to offer any alternate theory to the dreadful conjectures such things force upon the unwilling mind. There is no sense in such an attempt. I know now, of course, just what is meant by lycanthropy. I know how the old, discredited legends first came into being, on what desperately true phenomena they were based.

I do not know, I do not pretend to know, the exact mechanics of such dire transmutations of being as I unwillingly witnessed. I do not know how far the inner nature of man molds his body, the atoms of which are all thrown off and changed, replaced and altered in their entirety every seven years. I do not know to what extent the mere giving of one's self to evil may in rare instances effect the working out of alterations beyond anything we have ever suspected or dreamed of.

My personal theory is that Norn was from her birth one of those beings so utterly egoistic (Lucifer, star of the morning!) that she threw herself beyond the pale of common motives, common guidances and inspirations. We all blunder and sin, but deep in most of us is an occasional humility, a yearning desire to be better. To these, I believe Norn was a stranger.

Mr. Wolf was diffeent—how different, I shall never know. He was perhaps the product of some older race, some strange admixture of races, even—a sort of human chemical compound fraught with the dangers of a high explosive. He had lived in far parts of the world, become an adept of forbidden knowledge. He had tutored Norn, made her what he himself was—and, after her, Dorothy. The difference between the fox and the wolves was, I think, one of inherent, inborn characteristics. Little Dottie had been so innocent—yet not, perhaps, ever brilliant or over-strong of nature. She wasn't capable of the ferocities of those others—but, degraded and perverted by their machinations, she too slipped downward into that form of animal life she could achieve.

I gathered up and studied the shards of the container I had broken that night on the kitchen floor, and I know, of course, that the liquid it held, of which little Mary Rose drank before the change came upon her, must have been an essential part of the transmutation from human form into that of the beast. The light of the full moon also did its part. The characters and carving on the outer and inner curvatures of the shards were not very distinguishable, but in some way that I can not explain, they frightened me. I buried them—deep. And I have planted violets over the place where they are buried.

His
Brother's
Keeper

George Fielding Elliot

George Fielding Eliot

The most famous torture story in the English language is "The Copper Bowl" by Major George Fielding Eliot. It has been reprinted numerous times and, once read, is never forgotten. Eliot was a frequent contributor to all sorts of pulp magazines—aviation, sports and adventure—but he is remembered today for that one story. While "His Brother's Keeper" does not have quite the impact of the more famous work, it manages to chill the blood nicely in only a few pages. As Farnsworth Wright, so fond of puns, probably was tempted to proclaim, "A story short and to the point."

His Brother's Keeper

Major George Fielding Eliot

John Dangerfield was in love with his brother's fiancée—a position whose difficulties were somewhat ameliorated by the fact that from early childhood he had been accustomed to take away from his brother Horace any of Horace's possessions that he fancied; and oddly enough, he had always fancied what Horace cherished most.

Now he fancied Leslie Monroe—and that blonde young lady was by no means unconscious of the fact. Nor was she unconscious of the difference between being the wife of a younger son, a mere pensioner, and being the wife to the heir of Cragmore.

She stood now by John's side in a dusty room on the third story of an old brick warehouse, listening to the chatter of a gray little man in a skull-cap. The room was filled with odds and ends of every description, over which the gray little man waxed eloquent.

"This armor is really remarkable," the gray little man was saying. "But if you aren't interested in that, Mr. Dangerfield, here's something that will strike your fancy. It's the queerest thing I've had here for many a day; I found it in Nuremberg, and I've had it restored and put in good order."

He had paused before an object that looked like an up-ended sarcophagus. It was a little taller than a full-grown man, and entirely of iron. On its front it bore a bas-relief of a female figure; it was perhaps three feet wide, and twice as deep.

"Looks like a deep coffin stood on end," John Dangerfield remarked.

"Right!" the dealer replied. "Look here!"

He swung the back of the thing out on heavy hinges, like a door. At the bottom of this door was a stout shelf of iron; above this was fitted an assortment of iron bands, hinged and provided with locks. The dealer flashed the ray of a pocket torch into the dark interior; protruding back from its forward wall Leslie and Dangerfield saw six long, tapering iron spikes, glittering and sharp.

"This," the gray little man gloated, "is a genuine Iron Maiden! It is four hundred years old—built especially to the order of Duke Otho of Franconia. That whole front is movable; moves back into the box at the rate of about a half-inch every ten minutes; propelled by steel springs of incredible power. You put your victim against this door, standing on the shelf, and fasten him tight with the iron bands. The man can't move a muscle when they're all locked. Then you swing the door shut—so—putting your victim facing the spikes; a touch on this lever releases the mechanism, and the spikes move toward him. They're over a foot away to start with; gives him plenty of time to think over his sins! Note the spikes—the two bottom ones are the longest, and are supposed to pierce the groin or lower abdomen; then when they are well embedded, the next two pierce the shoulders; finally the last two pierce the poor devil's eyes, reach his brain at last and put him out of his misery. I fancy the whole process takes about six hours, from the time the machinery commences to move until the victim is dead."

"What a horrible, dreadful thing, John!" Leslie Monroe exclaimed. "Please take me away—I can't bear to look at it."

"Just as you say, dear," John Dangerfield answered tenderly. "We'll be going now, Nathan; I may be back to see you later."

"Monday, if you please, Mr. Dangerfield," the little gray man answered. "It's Saturday afternoon, sir; I'm closing up."

He opened the door leading to the dark landing. The man who had been so patiently waiting there in the shadows struck one savage blow and lowered the limp body of the dealer gently to the floor.

"What's the matter, Nathan?" John Dangerfield asked, hearing the thud of the blow. There was no answer; John in his turn stepped out upon the landing, and again the watcher in the shadows struck. The blackjack did its work well; John Dangerfield collapsed in a crumpled heap beside the dealer. The man who had struck him down stepped over his body into the storeroom to confront Leslie Monroe.

"Why, Horace!" she cried. "What are you—"

Then the light from the window fell full upon his face—his eyes—and Leslie Monroe fainted.

Horace Dangerfield laughed; the cunning, triumphant laugh of a madman.

"I've waited long," he muttered. "Too long—nothing has been adequate before. But this—this will do. This will satisfy me."

When John Dangerfield came to himself, he was in dust-filled darkness. He could not move, something was choking him—

Something was an iron collar, locked tight about his neck— his forehead was held back by an iron band—his wrists and ankles were in manacles—there was a dreadful clanking sound somewhere in the gloom.

Warm against his breast he felt living flesh—he realized that Leslie Monroe was there, bound tightly to him by straps or ropes; he spoke her name, but she did not answer.

The truth leaped upon John Dangerfield like a pouncing tiger. He was locked in the Iron Maiden, with Leslie Monroe bound before him so that the spikes would reach her first! He raised his voice:

"Help! Help!"

The words reverberated mockingly in that iron tomb; even more mockingly a voice from without answered.

"Cry again, John! There is no one to hear—save the Iron Maiden! I was listening last night when you told Leslie you wanted to be with her forever—even in death. You have your wish! Good-bye, John!"

"Horace, for the love of God—"

But only the sound of retreating feet and the slamming of a door answered. The machinery clanked again; and the first cruel touch of steel points revived the swooning Leslie.

The gloomy room rang with a woman's screams.

The Dead-Wagon

Greye La Spina

Greye La Spina

Every good horror anthology needs an old-fashioned melodramatic ghost story, and Greye La Spina's "The Dead Wagon" satisfies all the requirements. It contains all the ingredients that make such stories entertaining reading—an innocent child in peril, an ancient family curse, and sinister spirits who roam the darkest night. The authoress is best remembered for her short novel, "Invaders from the Dark," but this story and "The Devil's Pool" are her best works.

The Dead-Wagon

Greye La Spina

"Someone's been chalking up the front door." The speaker stepped off the terrace into the library through the open French window.

From his padded armchair Lord Melverson rose with an involuntary exclamation of startled dismay.

"Chalking the great door?" he echoed, an unmistakable tremor in his restrained voice. His aristocratic, clean-shaven old face showed pallid in the soft light of the shaded candles.

"Oh, nothing that can do any harm to the carving. Perhaps I am mistaken—it's coming on dusk—but it seemed to be a great cross in red, chalked high up on the top panel of the door. You know—the Great Plague panel."

"Good God!" ejaculated the older man weakly.

Young Dinsmore met his prospective father-in-law's anxious eyes with a face that betrayed his astonishment. He could not avoid marveling at the reception of what certainly seemed, on the surface, a trifling matter.

To be sure, the wonderfully carved door that, with reinforcement of hand-wrought iron, guarded the entrance to Melverson Abbey was well worth any amount of care. Lord Melverson's ill-concealed agitation would have been excusable had a tourist cut vandal initials on that admirable example of early carving. But to make such a fuss over a bit of red chalk that a servant could wipe off in a moment without injury to the panel—Kenneth felt slightly superior to such anxiety on the part of Arline's father.

Lord Melverson steadied himself with one hand against the library table.

"Was there—did you notice—anything else—besides the cross?"

"Why, I don't think there was anything else. Of course, I didn't look particularly. I had no idea you'd be so—interested," returned the young American.

"I think I'll go out and take a look at it myself. You may have imagined you saw some things, in the dusk,' murmured Lord Melverson, half to himself.

"May I come?'" inquired Dinsmore, vaguely disturbed at the very apparent discomposure of his usually imperturbable host.

Lord Melverson nodded. "I suppose you'll have to hear the whole story sooner or later, anyway," he acquiesced as he led the way.

His words set Kenneth's heart to beating madly. They meant but one thing: Arline's father was not averse to his suit. As for Arline, no one could be sure of such a little coquette. And yet— the young American could have sworn there was more than ordinary kindness in her eyes the day she smiled a confirmation of her father's invitation to Melverson Abbey. It was that vague promise that had brought Kenneth Dinsmore from New York to England.

A moment later, the American was staring, with straining eyes that registered utter astonishment, at the famous carved door that formed the principal entrance to the abbey. He would have been willing to swear that no one could have approached that door without having been seen from the library windows; yet in the few seconds of time that had elapsed between his first and second observation of the panel, an addition had been made to the chalk marks.

The Melverson panels are well known in the annals of historic carvings. There is a large lower panel showing the Great Fire of London. Above this are six half-panels portraying important scenes in London's history. And running across the very top is a large panel which shows a London street during the Great Plague of 1664.

This panel shows houses on either side of a narrow street yawning vacantly, great crosses upon their doors. Before one in the foreground is a rude wooden cart drawn by a lean nag and driven by a saturnine individual with leering face. This cart carries a gruesome load; it is piled high with bodies. Accounts vary oddly as to the number of bodies in the cart; earlier descriptions of the panel give a smaller number than the later ones, an item much speculated upon by connoisseurs of old carvings. The *tout ensemble* of the bas-relief greatly resembles the famous Hogarth picture of a similar scene.

Before this great door Kenneth stood, staring at a red-chalked legend traced across the rough surface of the carved figures on the upper panel. "God have mercy upon us!" it read. What did it mean? Who had managed to trace, unseen, those words of despairing supplication upon the old door?

And suddenly the young man's wonderment was rudely disturbed. Lord Melverson lurched away from the great door like a drunken man, a groan forcing its way from between his parched lips. The old man's hands had flown to his face, covering his eyes as though to shut out some horrid and unwelcome sight.

"Kenneth, you have heard the story! This is some thoughtless jest of yours! Tell me it is, boy! Tell me that your hand traced these fatal words!"

Dinsmore's sympathy was keenly aroused by the old nobleman's intense gravity and anxiety, but he was forced to deny the pitifully pleading accusation.

"Sorry, sir, but I found the red cross just as I told you. As for the writing below, I must admit—"

"Ah! Then you *did* put *that* there? It was you who did it, then? Thank God! Thank God!"

"No, no, I hadn't finished. I was only wondering how anyone could have slipped past us and have written this, unseen. I'm sure," puzzled, "there was nothing here but the red cross when I told you about it first, sir."

"Then you haven't heard—no one has told you that old legend? The story of the Melverson curse?"

"This is the first I've heard of it, I assure you."

"And you positively deny writing that, as a bit of a joke?"

"Come, sir, it's not like you to accuse me of such a silly piece of cheap trickery," Kenneth retorted, somewhat indignantly.

"Forgive me, boy. I—I should not have said that but—I am agitated. Will you tell me"—his voice grew tenser—"look closely, for God's sake, Kenneth!—*how many bodies are there in the wagon?*"

Dinsmore could not help throwing a keen glance at his future father-in-law, who now stood with averted face, one hand shielding his eyes as though he dared not ascertain for himself that which he asked another in a voice so full of shrinking dread. Then the American stepped closer to the door and examined the uper panel closely, while the soft dusk closed down upon it.

"There are eleven bodies," he said finally.

"Kenneth! Look carefully! More depends upon your reply than you can be aware. Are you sure there are only eleven?

"There are only eleven, sir   I'm positive of it."

"Don't make a mistake, for pity's sake!"

"Surely my eyesight hasn't been seriously impaired since this morning, when I bagged my share of birds," laughed the young man, in a vain effort to throw off the gloomy depression that seemed to have settled down upon him from the mere propinquity of the other.

"Thank God! Then there is still time," murmured the owner of the abbey brokenly, drawing a deep, shivering sigh of relief. "Let us return to the house, my boy." His voice had lost its usually light ironical inflection and had acquired a heaviness foreign to it.

Kenneth contracted his brows at Lord Melverson's dragging steps. One would almost have thought the old man physically affected by what appeared to be a powerful shock.

Once back in the library, Lord Melverson collapsed into the nearest chair, his breath coming in short, forced jerks. Wordlessly he indicated the bell-pull dangling against the wall out of his reach.

Kenneth jerked the cord. After a moment, during which the young man hastily poured a glassful of water and carried it to his host, the butler came into the room.

At sight of his beloved master in such a condition of pitiful collapse, the gray-haired old servitor was galvanized into action. He flew across the room to the desk, opened a drawer, picked up a bottle, shook a tablet out into his hand, flew back.

He administered the medicine to his master, who sipped the water brought by Kenneth with a grateful smile that included his guest and his servant.

Jenning shook his head sadly, compressing his lips, as Lord Melverson leaned back exhausted in his chair, face grayish, lids drooping over weary eyes.

Kenneth touched the old servant's arm to attract his attention. Then he tapped his left breast and lifted his eyebrows questioningly. An affirmative nod was his reply. Heart trouble! Brought on the by the old gentleman's agitation over a chalk mark on his front door! There was a mystery somewhere, and the very idea stimulated curiosity. And had not Lord Melverson said, "You will have to know, sooner or later"? Know what? What strange thing lay back of a red cross and a prayer to heaven, chalked upon the great Melverson portal?

2

Lord Melverson stirred ever so little and spoke with effort. "Send one of the men out to clean the upper panel of the front door, Jenning," he ordered tonelessly.

Jenning threw up one hand to cover his horrified mouth and stifle an exclamation. His faded blue eyes peered at his master from under pale eyebrows as he stared with dreadful incredulity.

"It isn't the red cross, m'lord? Oh, no, it cannot be the red cross?" he stammered.

The thrill of affection in that cracked old voice told a little something of how much his master meant to the old family retainer.

"It seems to be a cross, chalked in red," admitted Melverson with patent reluctance, raising dull eyes to the staring ones fixed upon him with consternation.

"Oh, m'lord, not the red cross! And—was the warning there? Yes? Did you count them? *How many were there?*"

Terrible foreboding, shrinking reluctance, rang in that inquiry, so utterly strange and incomprehensible. Kenneth felt his blood congeal in his veins with the horrid mystery of it.

Lord Melverson and his retainer exchanged a significant glance that did not escape the young American's attention. The answer to Jenning's question was cryptic but not more so than the inquiry.

""The same as before, Jenning. That is all—as yet."

Kenneth's curiosity flamed up anew. What could that mean? Could Jenning have been inquiring how many bodies were in the cart? There would be eleven, of course. How could there be more, or less, when the wood-carver had made them eleven, for all time?

The old servant retired from the room, dragging one slow foot after the other as though he had suddenly aged more than his fast-whitening hairs warranted.

In his capacious armchair, fingers opening and closing nervously upon the polished leather that upholstered it, Lord Melverson leaned back wearily, his eyes wide open but fixed unseeingly upon the library walls with their great paintings in oil of bygone Melversons.

"Kenneth!" Lord Melverson sought his guest's eyes with an expression of apology on his face that was painfully forced to the surface of the clouded atmosphere of dread and heaviness in which the old nobleman seemed steeped. "I presume you are wondering over the to-do about a chalk mark on my door? It—it made me think—of an old family tradition—and disturbed me a little.

"There's just one thing I want to ask you, my boy. Arline must not now that I had this little attack of heart-failure. I've kept it from her for years and I don't want her disturbed about me. And Kenneth, Arline has never been told the family legend. Don't tell her about the cross—the chalk marks on my door." His voice was intensely grave. "I have your word, my boy? Thank you. Some day I'll tell you the whole story."

"Has it anything to do with the quaint verse in raised gilded letters over the fireplace in the dining-hall?" questioned Kenneth.

He quoted it:

"Melverson's first-born will die early away;
 Melverson's daughters will wed in gray;
 Melverson's curse must Melverson pay,
 Or Melverson Abbey will ownerless stay."

"Sounds like doggerel, doesn't it, lad? Well, that's the ancient curse. Foolish? Perhaps it is—perhaps it is. Yet—I am a second son myself; my brother Guy died before his majority."

"Coincidence, don't you think, sir?"

Lord Melverson smiled wryly, unutterable weariness in his old eyes. "Possibly—but a chain of coincidences, then. You—you don't believe there could be anything in it, do you, Kenneth? Would you marry the daughter of a house with such a curse on it, knowing that it was part of your wife's dowry? Knowing that your first-born son must die before his majority?"

The American laughed light-heartedly.

"I don't think I'd care to answer such a supposititious question, sir. I can't admit such a possibility. I'm far too matter-of-fact, you see."

"But would you?" persistently, doggedly.

"I don't believe a word of it," sturdily. "It's just one of those foolish superstitions that people have permitted to influence them from time immemorial. I refuse to credit it."

Did Kenneth imagine it, or did Lord Melverson heave a deep, carefully repressed sigh of relief?

"Hardly worth while to go over the old tradition, is it?" he asked eagerly. "You wouldn't believe it, anyway. And probably it is just superstition, as you say. Ring for Jenning again, will you? Or—do you want to lend me your arm, my boy? I—I feel a bit shaky yet. I rather think bed will be the best place for me.

3

After Kenneth had bidden Lord Melverson good-night, he got out his pipe and sat by his window smoking. Tomorrow, he decided, he would try his fate; if he could only get Arline away where they could be alone. Little witch, how she managed always to have someone else around! Tomorrow he would know from her own lips whether or not he must return to America alone.

The clock struck midnight. Following close upon its cadences, a voice sounded on the still night, a voice raucous, grating, disagreeable. The words were indistinguishable and followed by a hard chuckle that was distinctly not expressive of mirth; far from it, the sound made Kenneth shake back his shoulders quickly in an instinctive effort to throw off the dismal effect of that laugh.

"Charming music!" observed he to himself, as he leaned from his window.

Wheels began to grate and crunch through the graveled road that led around the abbey. The full moon threw her clear light upon the space directly under Kenneth's window. He could distinguish every object as distinctly, it seemed to him, as in broad daylight. He listened and watched, a strange tenseness upon him. It was as though he waited for something terrible which yet must be; some unknown peril that threatened vaguely but none the less dreadfully.

The noise of the wheels grew louder. Then came a cautious, scraping sound from the window of a room close at hand. Kenneth decided that it was Lord Melverson's room. His host, hearing the horrid laughter that had been flung dismally upon the soft night air, had removed the screen from his window, the better to view the night visitor with the ugly chuckle.

The grinding of wheels grew louder. And then there slid into the full length of the moon a rude cart drawn by a lean, dappled nag and driven by a hunched-up individual who drew rein as the wagon came directly under Lord Melverson's window.

From the shadow of his room, Kenneth stared, open-eyed. There was something intolerably appalling about that strange equipage and its hunched-up driver, something that set his teeth sharply on edge and lifted his hair stiffly on his head. He did not want to look, but something pushed him forward and he was obliged to.

With a quick motion of his head, the driver turned a saturnine face to the moon's rays, revealing glittering eyes that shone with terrible, concentrated malignancy. The thinly curling lips parted. The cry Kenneth had heard a few minutes earlier rang—or rather, grated—on the American's ear. This time the words were plainer; plainer to the ear, although not to the sense—for what sense could they have? he reasoned as he heard them.

"Bring out your dead! Bring out your dead!"

A stifled groan. That was Lord Melverson, thought Kenneth, straining his eyes to watch the strange scene below.

For suddenly there rose from out the shadow of the abbey's great gray walls two figures bearing between them a burden. They carried it to the cart and with an effort lifted it, to toss it carelessly upon the grisly contents of that horrid wagon—contents that Kenneth now noted for the first time with starting eyes and prickling skin. And as the white face of the body lay upturned to the moon, a terrible cry wailed out from Lord Melverson's apartment, a cry of anguish and despair. For the moon's light picked out the features of that dead so callously tossed upon the gruesome pile.

"Oh, Albert, Albert, my son, my son!"

Kenneth leaned from his window and peered toward that of his host. From above the sill protruded two clasped hands; between them lay the white head of the old man. Had he fainted? Or had he had another attack of heart-failure?

The driver in the roadway below chuckled malignantly, and pulled at his horse's reins. The lean, dappled nag started up patiently in answer, and the cart passed slowly out of sight, wheels biting deep into the road-bed. And as it went out of sight among the deep shadows cast by the thickly wooded park, that harsh chuckle floated back again to the American's ears, thrilling him with horror of that detestable individual.

* * *

The hypnotic influence of that malignant glance had so chained Kenneth to the spot that for the moment he could not go to the assistance of Lord Melverson. But he found that he had been anticipated; as he reached his door, Jenning was already disappearing into his host's room. Kenneth retreated, unseen; perhaps he would do better to wait until he was called. It might well be that the drama he had seen enacted was not meant for his eyes and ears.

After all, had he seen or heard anything? Or was he the victim of a nightmare that had awakened him at its end? Kenneth shrugged his shoulders. He would know in the morning. Unless it rained hard in the meantime, the wheels of the cart would have left their mark on the gravel. If he had not dreamed, he would find the ruts made by those broad, ancient-looking wheels.

He could not sleep, however, until he heard Jenning leave his master's room. Opening the door softly, he inquired how Lord Melverson was. The old servitor flung a suspicious glance at him.

"I heard him cry out," explained Kenneth, seeing that the old man was averse to any explanation on his own side. "I hope it is nothing serious?"

"Nothing," replied Jenning restrainedly. But Dinsmore could have sworn that bright tears glittered in the old retainer's faded blue eyes and that the old mouth was compressed as though to hold back an outburst of powerful emotion.

Arline Melverson, her face slightly clouded, reported that her father had slept poorly the night before and would breakfast in his own room. She herself came down in riding-habit and vouchsafed the welcome information that she had ordered a horse saddled for Kenneth, if he cared to ride with her. Despite his desire to be alone with her, the American felt that he ought to remain at the abbey, where he might be of service to Lord Melverson. But inclination overpowered intuition, and after breakfast he got into riding-togs.

"I believe I'm still dreaming," he thought to himself as he rode back to the abbey at lunch-time, his horse crowding against Arline's as he reached happily over to touch her hand every little while. "Only this dream isn't a nightmare."

Instinctively his glance sought the graveled road where the dead-cart of the night before had, under his very eyes, ground its heavy wheels into the ground. The road was smooth and rutless. After all, then, he had dreamed and had undoubtedly been awakened by Lord Melverson's cry as the old man fainted. The dream had been so vivid that Kenneth could hardly believe his eyes when he looked at the smooth roadway, but his new happiness soon chased his bewilderment away.

As the young people dismounted before the door, Jenning appeared upon the threshold. The old man's lined face was turned almost with terror upon his young mistress. His lips worked as though he would speak but could not. His eyes sought the other mann's as if in supplication.

"What's the matter, Jenning?"

"Master Albert, Mr. Dinsmore! M'lord's first-born son!"

"What is it?" Arline echoed. "Is my brother here?"

"I can't tell her, sir," the major-domo implored of Kenneth. "Take her to Lord Melverson, sir, I beg of you. He can tell her better than I."

Kenneth did not take Arline to her father. The girl fled across the great hall as if whipped by a thousand fears. Kenneth turned to Jenning with a question in his eyes.

Down the old man's face tears ran freely. His wrinkled hands worked nervously together. "He fell, sir. Something broke on his plane. He died last night, sir, a bit after midnight. The telegram came this morning, just after you and Miss Arline went."

Kenneth, one hand pressed bewildered to his forehead, walked aimlessly through that house of sorrow. Albert Melverson had fallen from his plane and died, the previous night. Had that dream, that nightmare, been a warning? Had it perhaps been so vivid in Lord Melverson's imagination that the scene had been telepathically reproduced before the American's own eyes?

Although puzzled and disturbed beyond words, Kenneth realized that the matter must rest in abeyance until Lord Melverson should of his own free will explain it.

In the meantime there would be Arline to comfort, his sweetheart, who had just lost her dearly beloved and only brother.

4

Two months had hardly passed after Albert's death before Lord Melverson broached the subject of his daughter's marriage.

"It's this way, my boy. I'm an old man and far from well of late. I'd like to know that Arline was in safe keeping, Kenneth," and he laid an affectionate hand on the young man's shoulder.

Kenneth was deeply affected. "Thank you, sir. I promise you I shall do my utmost to make her happy."

"I know you will. I want you to speak to Arline about an early wedding. Tell her I want to see her married before—before I have to leave. I have a very powerful reason that I cannot tell you, my boy, for Arline to marry soon. I want to live to see my grandson at her knee, lad. And unless you two marry soon, I shall be powerless to prevent—that is, I shall be unable to do something for you both that has been much in my mind of late. It is vital that you marry soon, Kenneth. More I cannot say."

"You don't need to say more. I'll speak to Arline today. You understand, sir, that my only motive in not urging marriage upon her now has been your recent bereavement?"

"Of course. But Arline is too young, too volatile, to allow even such a loss to weigh permanently upon her spirits. I think she will yield to you, especially if you make it plain that I want it to be so."

Kenneth sought Arline thoughtfully. Lord Melverson's words impressed him almost painfully. There was much behind them, much that he realized he could not yet demand an explanation of. But the strength of Lord Melverson's request made him surer when he asked Arline to set an early date for their marriage.

"I am ready if Father does not consider it disrespectful to Albert's memory, Kenneth. You know, dear, we intended to marry soon, anyway. And I think Albert will be happier to know that I did not let his going matter. You understand, don't you? Besides, I feel that he is here with us in the abbey, with Father and me.

"But there is one thing, dear, that I shall insist upon. I think too much of my brother to lay aside the light mourning that Father permitted me to wear instead of heavy black. So if you want me to marry you soon, dear, you must wed a bride in gray."

Into Kenneth's mind flashed one line of the Melverson curse: *"Melverson's daughters will wed in gray."*

Could there be something in it, after all? Common sense answered scornfully: No!

Four months after Albert Melverson had fallen to his death, his sister Arline—gray-clad like a gentle dove—put her hand into that of Kenneth Dinsmore, while Lord Melverson, his lips twitching as he strove to maintain his composure, gave the bride away.

A honeymoon trip that consumed many months took the young people to America as well as to the Continent, as the groom could hardly wait to present his lovely young wife to his family. Then, pursuant to Lord Melverson's wishes, the bridal pair returned to Melverson Abbey, that the future heir might be born under the ancestral roof.

5

Little Albert became the apple of his grandfather's eye. The old gentleman spent hours watching the cradle the first few months of his grandson's life, and then again other hours in fondly guiding the little fellow's first steps.

But always in the background of this apparently ideally happy family lurked a black shadow. Jenning, his pale eyes full of foreboding, was always stealing terrified looks in secret at the panel of the great door. Kenneth grew almost to hate the poor old man, merely because he knew that Jenning believed implicitly in the family curse.

"Confound the man! He'll bring it upon us by thinking about it," growled the young father one morning as he looked out of the window of the breakfast room, where he had been eating a belated meal.

Little Albert, toddling with exaggerated precaution from his mother's outstretched hands to those of his grandfather, happened to look up. He saw his father; laughed and crowed lustily. Dinsmore waved his hand.

"Go to it, young chap. You'll be a great walker some day," he called facetiously.

Lord Melverson looked around, a pleased smile on his face. Plainly, he agreed to the full with his son-in-law's sentiments.

As usual, entered that black-garbed figure, the presentment of woe: Jenning. Into the center of the happy little circle he came, his eyes seeking the old nobleman's.

"M'lord! Would your lordship please take a look?" stammered Jenning, his roving eyes going from the young father to the young mother, then back to the grandfather again, as if in an agony of uncertainty.

Lord Melverson straightened up slowly and carefully from his bent position over the side of a great wicker chair. He motioned Jenning silently ahead of him. The old butler retraced his footsteps, his master following close upon his heels. They disappeared around the corner of the building.

"Now, what on earth are they up to?" wondered Kenneth. His brow contracted. There had been something vaguely suspicious about Lord Melverson's air. "I've half a mind to follow them."

"Kenneth!" Arline's cry was wrung agonizingly from her.

Kenneth whirled about quickly, but too late to do anything. The baby, toddling to his mother's arms, missed a step, slipped, fell. The tender little head crashed against the granite coping at the edge of the terrace.

And even then Kenneth did not realize what it all meant. It was not until late that night that he suddenly understood that the Melverson curse was not silly tradition, but a terrible blight upon the happiness of the Melverson family, root and branch.

He had left Arline under the influence of a sleeping-potion. Her nerves had gone back on her after the day's strain and the knowledge that her baby might not live out the night. A competent nurse and a skilled physician had taken over the case. Specialists were coming down from London as fast as a special train would bring them. Kenneth felt that his presence in the sickroom would be more hindrance than help.

He went down to the library where his father-in-law sat grimly, silently, expectantly, a strangely fixed expression of determination on his fine old face. Lord Melverson had drawn a handkerchief from his pocket. And then Kenneth suddenly knew, where before he had only imagined. For the old man's fine cambric kerchief was streaked with red, red that the unhappy young father knew must have been wiped from the upper panel of the great door that very morning. *The baby, Kenneth's first-born son, was doomed.*

"Why didn't you tell me? You hid it from me." he accused his wife's father, bitterly.

"I thought I was doing it for the best, Kenneth," the older man defended himself sadly.

"But if you had told me, I would never have left him alone for a single moment. I would have been beside him to have saved him when he fell."

"You *know* that if he had not fallen, something else would have happened to him, something unforeseen."

"Oh yes, I know, now, when it is too late. My little boy! My Arline's first-born! The first-born of Melverson!" fiercely. "Why didn't you tell me that the Melverson curse would follow my wife? That it would strike down her first-born boy?"

"And would that have deterred you from marrying Arline?" inquired Arline's father, very gently. "You know it wouldn't, Kenneth. I tried to put a hypothetical case to you once, but you replied that you refused to consider the mere possibility. What was I to do? I will confess that I have suffered, thinking that I should have insisted upon your reading the family records before you married Arline—then you could have decided for yourself."

"Does Arline know?"

"No. I've shielded her from the knowledge, Kenneth."

"I can't forgive you for not letting me know. It might have saved Albert's life. If Arline, too, had known—"

"Why should I have told her something that would have cast a shadow over her young life, Kenneth? Are you reproaching me because I have tried to keep her happy?"

"Oh, Father, I didn't mean to reproach you. I'm sorry. You must understand that I'm half mad with the pain of what's happened, not only on account of the little fellow, but for Arline. Oh, if there were only some way of saving him! How I would bless the being who would tell me how to save him!"

Lord Melverson, still with that strange glow in his eyes, rose slowly to his feet.

"There is a way, I believe," said he. "But don't put too much stress on what may be but a groundless hope on my part. I have had an idea for some time that I shall put into expression tonight, Kenneth. I've been thinking it over since I felt that I had wronged you in not pressing home the reality of the Melverson curse. If my idea is a good one, our little Albert is saved. And not only he, but I too shall have broken the curse, rendered it impotent for ever." His eyes shone with fervor.

"Is it anything I can do?" the young father begged.

"Nothing. Unless, perhaps, you want to read the old manuscript in my desk drawer. It tells why we Melversons have been cursed since the days of the Great Plague of 1664.

"Just before midnight, be in little Albert's room. If he is no better when the clock strikes twelve, Kenneth—why, then, my plan will have been a poor one. But I shall have done all I can do; have given all that lies in my power to give, in my attempt to wipe out the wrong I have inadvertently done you."

Kenneth pressed the hand outstretched to him.

"You've been a good husband to my girl, Kenneth, lad. You've made her happy. And, in case anything were to happen to me, will you tell Arline that I am perfectly contented if only our little one recovers? I want no vain regrets," stressed Lord Melverson emphatically, as he released Kenneth's hand and turned to leave the room.

"What could happen?"

"Oh, nothing. That is—you know I've had several severe heart attacks of late," returned Arline's father vaguely.

6

Kenneth, alone, went to his father-in-law's desk and drew out the stained and yellow manuscript. Sitting in a chair before the desk, he laid the ancient sheets before him and pored over the story of the Melverson curse. He thought it might take his mind off the tragedy slowly playing to a close in the hushed room upstairs.

Back in 1664, the then Lord Melverson fell madly in love with the charming daughter of a goldsmith. She was an only child, very lovely to look upon and as good as she was fair, and she dearly loved the rollicking young nobleman. But a Melverson of Melverson Abbey, though he could love, could not wed a child of the people. Charles Melverson pleaded with the lovely girl to elope with him, without the sanction of her church.

But the damsel, being of lofty soul, called her father and related all to him. Then she turned her fair shoulder indifferently upon her astonished and chagrined suitor and left him, while the goldsmith laughed saturninely in the would-be seducer's face.

A Melverson was not one to let such a matter rest quietly, however, especially as he was deeply enamored of the lady. He sent pleading letters, threatening to take his own life. He attempted to force himself into the lady's presence. At last, he met her one day as she returned from church, caught her up, and fled with her on his swift charger.

Still she remained obdurate, although love for him was eating her wounded heart. Receive him she must, but she continued to refuse him so little a favor as a single word.

Despairing of winning her by gentle means, Charles Melverson determined upon foul.

It was the terrible winter of 1664-5. The Black Death, sweeping through London and out into the countryside, was taking dreadful toll of lives. Hundreds of bodies were daily tumbled carelessly into the common trenches by hardened men who dared the horrors of the plague for the big pay offered those who played the part of grave-digger. And at the very moment when Melverson had arrived at his evil decision, the goldsmith staggered into the abbey grounds after a long search for his ravished daughter, to fall under the very window where she had retreated in the last stand for her maiden virtue.

Retainers without shouted at one another to beware the plague-stricken man. Their shouts distracted the maiden. She looked down and beheld her father dying, suffering the last throes of the dreaded pestilence.

Coldly and proudly she demanded freedom to go down to her dying parent. Melverson refused the request; in a flash of insight he knew what she would do with her liberty. She would fling herself desperately beside the dying man; she would hold his blackening body against her own warm young breast; she would deliberately drink in his plague-laden breath with her sweet, fresh lips.

Lifting fast-glazing eyes, the goldsmith saw his daughter, apparently clasped fast in her lover's arms. How was he to have known that her frantic struggles had been in vain? With his last breath he cursed the Melversons, root and branch, lifting discolored hands to the brazen, glowing sky lowering upon him. Then, "And may the demon of the plague grant that I may come back as long as a Melverson draws breath, to steal away his first-born son!" he cried, With a groan, he died.

And then, thanks to the strange heart of woman, Charles Melverson unexpectedly won what he had believed lost to him for ever, for he could not have forced his will upon that orphaned and sorrowful maiden. The goldsmith's daughter turned upon him limpid eyes that wept for him and for her father, too.

"It is too much to ask that you should suffer alone what my poor father has called down upon your house," she said to him, with unexpected gentleness. "He would forgive you, could he know that I have been safe in your keeping. I must ask you, then, to take all I have to give, if by so doing you believe the shadow of the curse will be lightened—for you, at least."

Touched to his very heart by her magnanimity, Charles Melverson released her from his arms, knelt at her feet, kissed her hand, and swore that until he could fetch her from the church, his lawful wedded wife, he would neither eat nor sleep.

But—the curse remained. Down through the centuries it had worked its evil way, and no one seemed to have found a way of eluding it. Upon the last pages of the old manuscript were noted, in differing chirography, the death dates of one Melverson after another, after each the terribly illuminating note: "First-born son. Died before his majority."

And last of all, in the handwriting of Lord Melverson, was written the name of that Albert for whom Kenneth Dinsmore's son had been named. Must another Albert follow that other so soon?

7

Kenneth tossed the stained papers back into the drawer and shut them from sight. There was something sinister about them. He felt as if his very hands had been polluted by their touch. Then he glanced at the clock. It was on the point of striking midnight. He remembered Lord Melverson's request, and ran quickly upstairs to his little dying son's room.

Arline was already at the child's side; she had wakened and would not be denied. Nurse and physician stood in the background, their faces showing plainly the hopelessness of the case.

On his little pillow, the poor baby drew short, painful gasps, little fists clenched against his breast. A few short moments, thought Kenneth, would determine his first-born's life or death. And it would be death, unless Lord Melverson had discovered how to break the potency of the Melverson curse.

Torn between wife and child, the young father dared not hope, for fear his hope might be shattered. As for Arline, he saw that her eyes already registered despair; already she had, in anticipation, given up her child, her baby, her first-born.

What was that? The sound of heavy, broad-rimmed wheels crunching through the gravel of the roadway; the call of a mocking voice that set Kenneth's teeth on edge with impotent fury.

He went unobtrusively to the window and looked out. After all, he could not be expected to stand by the bed, watching his little son die. And he had to see, at all costs, that nightmare dead-cart with its ghastly freight; he had to know whether or not he had dreamed it, or had seen it truly, on the night before Albert Melverson's death.

Coming out of the shadows of the enveloping trees, rumbled the dead-wagon with its hunched-up driver. Kenneth's hair rose with a prickling sensation on his scalp. He turned to glance back into the room. No, he was not dreaming; he had not dreamed before; it was real—as real as such a ghastly thing could well be.

On, on it came. And then the hateful driver lifted his malignant face to the full light of the moon. His challenging glance met the young father's intent gaze with a scoffing, triumphant smile, a smile of satisfied hatred. The thin lips parted, and their grating cry fell another time upon the heavy silence of the night.

"Bring out your dead!"

As that ominous cry pounded against his ears, Kenneth Dinsmore heard yet another sound: it was the sharp explosion of a revolver.

He stared from the window with straining eyes. Useless to return to the baby's bedside; would not those ghostly pall-bearers emerge from the shadows now, bearing with them the tiny body of his first-born?

They came, But they were carrying what seemed to be a heavy burden. That was no child's tiny form they tossed with hideous upward grins upon the dead-cart.

"Kenneth! Come here!"

It was Arline's voice, with a thrilling undertone of thankfulness in it that whirled Kenneth fromn the window to her side, all else forgotten.

"Look! He is breathing easier. Doctor, look! Tell me, doesn't he seem better?"

Doctor and nurse exchanged mystified, incredulous glances. It was plain that neither had heard or seen anything out of the ordinary that night, but that the baby's sudden turn for the better had astonished them both.

"I consider it little short of a miracle," pronounced the medical man, after a short examination of the sleeping child. "Madam, your child will live. I congratulate you both."

"Oh, I must tell Father, Kenneth. He will be *so* happy. Dear Father!"

The cold hand of certain knowlege squeezed Kenneth's heart. "If anything should happen to me," Lord Melverson had said. What did that revolver shot mean? What had meant that body the ghostly pall-bearers had carried to the dead-wagon?

A light tap came at the door. The nurse opened it, then turned and beckoned to Kenneth.

"He's gone, Mr. Dinsmore. Break it to her easy, sir—but it's proud of him she ought to be." His voice trembled, broke. "Twas not the little master *they* carried away in the accursed dead-cart, thanks to him. I tried to stop him, sir; forgive me, I loved him! But he *would* make the sacrifice; he said it was worth trying. And so— he—did—it. But—*he's broken the curse, sir, he's broken the curse!*"

The
Floor
Above

M.L. Humphreys

M.L. Humphreys

The early issues of Weird Tales *contain a number of stories by authors who only appeared one time in the "Unique Magazine." Loural Sugarman was one such writer. M.L. Humphreys was another. Lovecraft had high praise for "The Floor Above" and from the quality of the writing, it seems hard to believe, this was the author's only professional work.*

The Floor Above

M.L. HUMPHREYS

September 17, 1922.—I sat down to breakfast this morning with a good appetite. The heat seemed over, and a cool wind blew in from my garden, where chrysanthemums were already budding. The sunshine streamed into the room and fell pleasantly on Mrs. O'Brien's broad face as she brought in the eggs and coffee. For a supposedly lonely old bachelor the world seemed to me a pretty good place. I was buttering my third set of waffles when the housekeeper again appeared, this time with the mail.

I glanced carelessly at the three or four letters beside my plate. One of them bore a stangely familiar handwriting. I gazed at it a minute, then seized it with a beating heart. Tears almost came into my eyes. There was no doubt about it—it was Arthur Barker's handwriting! Shaky and changed, to be sure, but ten years have passed since I have seen Arthur, or, rather, since his mysterious disappearance.

For ten years I have not had a word from him. His people know no more than I what has become of him, and long ago we gave him up for dead. He vanished without leaving a trace behind him. It seemed to me, too, that with him vanished the last shreds of my youth. For Arthur was my dearest friend in that happy time. We were boon companions, and many a mad prank we played together.

And now, after ten years of silence, Arthur was writing to me!

The envelope was postmarked Baltimore. Almost reluctantly—for I feared what it might contain—I passed my finger under the flap and opened it. It held a single sheet of paper torn from a pad. But it was Arthur's writing:

Dear Tom:
"Old man, can you run down to see me for a few days? I'm afraid I'm in a bad way.
"Arthur."

119

Scrawled across the bottom was the address, 536 N. Marathon Street.

I have often visited Baltimore, but I can not recall a street of that name.

Of course I shall go... But what a strange letter after ten years! There is something almost uncanny about it.

I shall go tomorrow evening. I can not possibly get off before then.

September 18—I am leaving tonight. Mrs. O'Brien has packed my two suitcases, and everything is in readiness for my departure. Ten minutes ago I handed her the keys and she went off tearfully. She has been sniffling all day and I have been perplexed, for a curious thing occurred this morning.

It was about Arthur's letter. Yesterday, when I had finished reading it, I took it to my desk and placed it in a small compartment together with other personal papers. I remember distinctly that it was on top, with a lavender card from my sister directly underneath. This morning I went to get it. It was gone.

There was the lavender card exactly where I had seen it, but Arthur's letter had completely disappeared. I turned everything upside down, then called Mrs. O'Brien and we both searched, but in vain. Mrs. O'Brien, in spite of all I could say, took it upon herself to feel that I suspected her... But what could have become of it? Fortunately I remembered the address.

September 19—I have arrived. I have seen Arthur. Even now he is in the next room and I am supposed to be preparing for bed. But something tells me I shall not sleep a wink this night. I am strangely wrought up, though there is not the shadow of an excuse for my excitement. I should be rejoicing to have found my friend again. And yet—

I reached Baltimore this morning at eleven o'clock. The day was warm and beautiful, and I loitered outside the station a few minutes before calling a taxi. The driver seemed well acquainted with the street I gave him, and we rolled off across the bridge.

As I drew near my destination, I began to feel anxious and afraid. But the ride lasted longer than I expected—Marathon Steet seemed to be located in the suburbs of the city. At last we turned into a dusty street, paved only in patches and lined with linden and aspen trees. The fallen leaves crunched beneath the tires. The September sun beat down with a white intensity. The taxi drew up before a house in the middle of a block that boasted not more than six dwellings. One each side of the house was a vacant lot, and it was set far back at the end of a long narrow yard crowded with trees.

I paid the driver, opened the gate and went in. The trees were so thick that not until I was half-way up the path did I get a good view of the house. It was three stories high, built of brick, in fairly good repair, but lonely and deserted-looking. The blinds were closed in all of the windows with the exception of two, one on the first, one on the second floor. Not a sign of life anywhere, not a cat nor a milk-bottle to break the monotony of leaves that carpeted the porch.

But, overcoming my feeling of uneasiness, I resolutely set my suitcases on the porch, caught at the old-fashioned bell, and gave an energetic jerk. A startling peal jangled through the silence. I waited, but there was no answer.

After a minute I rang again. Then from the interior I heard a queer dragging sound, as if some one was coming slowly down the hall. The knob was turned and the door opened. I saw before me an old woman, wrinkled, withered, and filmy-eyed, who leaned on a crutch.

"Does Mr. Barker live here?" I asked.

She nodded, staring at me in a curious way, but made no move to invite me in.

"Well, I've come to see him," I said. "I'm a friend of his. He sent for me."

At that she drew slightly aside.

"He's upstairs," she said in a cracked voice that was little more than a whisper. "I can't show you up. Hain't been up a stair now in ten years."

"That's all right," I replied, and, seizing my suitcases, I strode down the long hall.

"At the head of the steps," came the whispering voice behind me. "The door at the end of the hall."

I climbed the cold dark stairway, passed along the sort hall at the top, and stood before a closed door. I knocked.

"Come in." It was Arthur's voice, and yet—not his.

I opened the door and saw Arthur sitting on a couch, his shoulders hunched over, his eyes raised to mine.

After all, ten years had not changed him so much. As I remembered him, he was of medium height, inclined to be stout, and ruddy-faced, with keen gray eyes. He was still stout, but had lost his color and his eyes had dulled.

"And where have you been all this time?" I demanded, when the first greetings were over.

"Here," he answered.

"In this house?"

"Yes."

"But why didn't you let us hear from you?"

He seemed to be making an effort to speak.

"What did it matter? I didn't suppose any one cared."

Perhaps it was my imagination, but I could not get rid of the thought that Arthur's pale eyes, fixed tenaciously upon my face, were trying to tell me something, something quite different from what his lips said.

I felt chilled. Although the blinds were open, the room was almost darkened by the branches of the trees that pressed against the window. Arthur had not given me his hand, had seemed troubled to know how to make me welcome. Yet of one thing I was certain: He needed me and he wanted me to know he needed me.

As I took a chair I glanced about the room. It was a typical lodging-house room, medium-sized, with flowered wallpaper, worn matting, nondescript rugs, a wash-stand in one corner, a chiffonier in another, a table in the center, two or three chairs, and the couch which evidently served Arthur as a bed. But it was cold, strangely cold for such a warm day.

Arthur's eyes had wandered uneasily to my suitcases. He made an effort to drag himself to his feet.

"Your room is back here," he said, with a motion of his thumb.

"No, wait," I protested. "Let's talk about yourself first. What's wrong?"

"I've been sick."

"Haven't you a doctor? If not, I'll get one."

At this he started up with the first sign of animation he had shown.

"No, Tom, don't do it. Doctors can't help me now. Besides, I hate them. I'm afraid of them."

His voice trailed away, and I took pity on his agitation. I decided to let the question of doctors drop for the moment.

"As you say," I assented carelessly.

Without more ado, I followed him into my room, which adjoined his and was furnished in much the same fashion. But there were two windows, one on each side, looking out on the vacant lots. Consequently there was more light, for which I was thankful. In a far corner I noticed a door, heavily bolted.

"There's one more room," said Arthur, as I deposited my belongings, "one that you'll like. But we'll have to go through the bathroom."

Groping our way through the musty bathroom, in which a tiny jet of gas was flickering, we stepped into a large, almost luxurious chamber. It was a library, well-furnished, carpeted, and surrounded by shelves fairly bulging with books. But for the chillness and bad light, it was perfect. As I moved about, Arthur followed me with his eyes.

"There are some rare works on botany—"

I had already discovered them, a set of books that I would have given much to own. I could not contain my joy.

"You won't be so bored browsing around in here—"

In spite of my preoccupation, I pricked up my ears. In that monotonous voice there was no sympathy with my joy. It was cold and tired.

When I had satisfied my curiosity we returned to the front room, and Arthur flung himself, or rather fell, upon the couch. It was nearly five o'clock and quite dark. As I lighted the gas, I heard a sound below as of somebody thumping on the wall.

"That's the old woman," Arthur explained. "She cooks my meals, but she's too lame to bring them up."

He made a feeble attempt at rising, but I saw he was worn out.

"Don't stir," I warned him. "I'll bring up your food tonight."

To my surprise, I found the dinner appetizing and well-cooked, and, in spite of the fact that I did not like the looks of the old woman, I ate with relish. Arthur barely touched a few spoonfuls of soup to his lips and absently crumbled some bread in his plate.

Directly I had carried off the dishes, he wrapped his reddish-brown dressing gown about him, stretched out at full length on the couch, and asked me to turn out the gas. When I had complied with his request, I again heard his weak voice asking if I had everything I needed.

"Everything," I assured him, and then there was unbroken silence.

I went to my room, finally, closed the door, and here I am sitting restlessly between the two back windows that look out on the vacant lots.

I have unpacked my clothes and turned down the bed, but I can not make up my mind to retire. If the truth be told, I hate to put out the light. . . . There is something disturbing in the way the dry leaves tap on the panes. And my heart is sad when I think of Arthur.

I have found my old friend, but he is no longer my old friend. Why does he fix his pale eyes so strangely on my face? What does he wish to tell me?

But these are morbid thoughts. I will put them out of my head. I will go to bed and get a good night's rest. And tomorrow I will wake up finding everything right and as it should be.

September 26—I have been here a week today, and have settled down to this queer existence as if I had never known another. The day after my arrival I discovered that the third volume of the botanical series was done in Latin, which I have set myself the task of translating. It is absorbing work, and when I have buried myself in one of the deep chairs by the library table, the hours fly fast.

For health's sake I force myself to walk a few miles every day. I have tried to prevail on Arthur to do likewise, but he, who used to be so active, now refuses to budge from the house. No wonder he is literally blue! For it is a fact that his complexion, and the shadows about his eyes and temples, are decidedly blue.

What does he do with himself all day? Whenever I enter his room, he is lying on the couch, a book beside him, which he never reads. He does not seem to suffer pain, for he never complains. After several ineffectual attempts to get medical aid for him, I have given up mentioning the subject of doctor. I feel that his trouble is more mental than physical.

September 28—A rainy day. It has been coming down in floods since dawn. And I got a queer turn this afternoon.

As I could not get out for my walk, I spent the morning staging a general house-cleaning. It was time! Dust and dirt everywhere. The bathroom, which has no window and is lighted by gas, was fairly overrun with water-bugs and roaches. Of course I did not penetrate to Arthur's room, but I heard no sound from him as I swept and dusted.

I made a good dinner and settled down in the library, feeling quite cozy. The rain came down steadily and it had grown so cold I decided to make a fire later on. But once I had gathered my tablets and notebooks about me I forgot the cold.

I remember I was on the subject of the *Aster trifolium,* a rare variety seldom found in this country. Turning a page, I came upon a specimen of this very variety, dried, pressed flat, and pasted to the margin. Above it, in Arthur's handwriting, I read: *September 27, 1912.*

I was bending close to examine it, when I felt a vague fear. It seemed to me that some one was in the room and was watching me. Yet I had not heard the door open, nor seen any one enter. I turned sharply and saw Arthur, wrapped in his reddish-brown dressing-gown, standing at my very elbow.

He was smiling—smiling for the first time since my arrival, and his dull eyes were bright. But I did not like that smile. In spite of myself I jerked away from him. He pointed at the aster.

"It grew in the front yard under a linden tree. I found it yesterday."

"Yesterday!" I shouted, my nerves on edge. "Good Lord, man! Look! It was ten years ago!"

The smile faded from his face.

"Ten years ago," he repeated thickly. *"Ten years ago?"*

•   •   •

Five o'clock. Dusk is falling. O God! What has come over me? Am I the same man that went out of this house three hours ago? And what has happened? . . .

I had a splendid walk, and was striding homeward in a fine glow. But as I turned the corner and came in sight of the house, it was as if I looked at death itself. I could hardly drag myself up the stairs, and when I peered into the shadowy chamber, and saw the man hunched up on the couch, with his eyes fixed intently on my face, I could have screamed like a woman. I wanted to fly, to rush out into the clear cold air and run—to run and never come back! But I controlled myself, forced my feet to carry me to my room.

There is a weight of hopelessness at my heart. The darkness is advancing, swallowing up everything, but I have not the will to light the gas. . . .

Now there is a flicker in the front room. I am a fool; I must pull myself together. Arthur is lighting up, and downstairs I can hear the thumping that announces dinner. . . .

It is a queer thought that comes to me now, but it is odd I have not noticed it before. We are about to sit down to our evening meal. Arthur will eat practically nothing, for he has no appetite. Yet he remains stout. It can not be healthy fat, but even at that it seems to me that a man who eats as little as he does would become a living skeleton.

October 5—Positively, I must see a doctor about myself, or soon I shall be a nervous wreck. I am acting like a child. Last night I lost all control and played the coward.

I had gone to bed early, tired out from a hard day's work. It was raining again, and as I lay in bed I watched the little rivulets trickling down the panes. Lulled by the sighing of the wind among the leaves, I feel asleep.

I awoke (how long afterward I can not say) to feel a cold hand laid on my arm. For a moment I lay paralyzed with terror. I would have cried aloud, but I had no voice. At last I managed to sit up, to shake the hand off. I reached for the matches and lighted the gas.

It was Arthur who stood by my bed—Arthur wrapped in his eternal reddish- brown dressing-gown. He was excited. His blue face had a yellow tinge, and his eyes gleamed in the light.

"Listen!" he whispered

I listened but heard nothing.

"Don't you hear it?" he gasped, and he pointed upward.

"Upstairs?" I stammered. "Is there somebody upstairs?"

I strained my ears, and at last I fancied I could hear a fugitive sound like the light tapping of footsteps.

"It must be somebody walking about up there," I suggested.

"No!" he cried in a sharp rasping voice. "No! It is nobody walking about up there!"

And he fled into his room.

For a long time I lay trembling, afraid to move. But at last, fearing for Arthur, I got up and crept to his door. He was lying on the couch, with his face in the moonlight, apparently asleep.

October 6—I had a talk with Arthur today. Yeserday I could not bring myself to speak of the previous night's happening, but all of this nonsense must be cleared away.

We were in the library. A fire was burning in the grate, and Arthur had his feet on the fender. The slippers he wears are as objectionable to me as his dressing-gown. They are felt slippers, old and worn, and frayed around the edges as if they had been gnawed by rats. I can not imagine why he does not get a new pair.

"Say, old man," I began abruptly, "do you own this house?"

He nodded.

"Don't you rent any of it?"

"Downstairs—to Mrs. Harlan."

"But upstairs?"

He hesitated, then shook his head.

"No, it's inconvenient. There's only a peculiar way to get upstairs."

I was struck by this.

"By Jove! you're right. Where's the staircase?"

He looked me full in the eyes.

"Don't you remember seeing a bolted door in a corner of your room? The staircase runs from that door."

I did remember it, and somehow the memory made me uncomfortable. I said no more and decided not to refer to what had happened that night. It occurred to me that Arthur might have been walking in his sleep.

October 8—When I went for my walk on Tuesday I dropped in and saw Doctor Lorraine, who is an old friend. He expressed some surprise at my rundown condition and wrote me a prescription.

I am planning to go home next week. How pleasant it will be to walk in my garden and listen to Mrs. O'Brien singing in the kitchen!

October 9—Perhaps I had better postpone my trip. I casually mentioned it to Arthur this morning.

He was lying relaxed on the sofa, but when I spoke of leaving he sat up as straight as a bolt. His eyes fairly blazed.

"No, Tom, don't go!" There was terror in his voice, and such pleading that it wrung my heart.

"You've stood it alone here ten years," I protested. "And now—"

"It's not that," he said. "But if you go, you will never come back."

"Is that all the faith you have in me?"

"I've got faith, Tom. But if you go, you'll never come back."

I decided that I must humor the vagaries of a sick man.

"All right," I agreed. "I'll not go. Anyway, not for some time."

October 12—What is it that hangs over this house like a cloud? For I can no longer deny that there *is* something—something indescribably oppressive. It seems to pervade the whole neighborhood.

Are all the houses on this block vacant? If not, why do I never see children playing in the street? Why are passers-by so rare?

And why, when from the front window I do catch a glimpse of one, is he hastening away as fast as possible?

I am feeling blue again. I know that I need a change, and this morning I told Arthur definitely that I was going.

To my surprise, he made no objection. In fact, he murmured a word of assent and smiled. He smiled as he smiled in the library that morning when he pointed at the *Aster trifolium*. And I don't like that smile. Anyway, it is settled. I shall go next week, Thursday, the 19th.

October 13—I had a strange dream last night. Or was it a dream? It was so vivid. . . . All day long I have been seeing it over and over again.

In my dream I thought that I was lying there in my bed. The moon was shining brightly into the room, so that each piece of furniture stood out distinctly. The bureau is so placed that when I am lying on my back, with my head high on the pillow, I can see full into the mirror.

I thought I was lying in this manner and staring into the mirror. In this way I saw the bolted door in the far corner of the room. I tried to keep my mind off it, to think of something else, but it drew my eyes like a magnet.

It seemed to me that some one was in the room, a vague figure that I could not recognize. It approached the door and caught at the bolts. It dragged at them and struggled, but in vain—they would not give way.

Then it turned and showed me its agonized face. It was Arthur! I recognized his reddish-brown dressing-gown.

I sat up in bed and cried to him, but he was gone. I ran to his room, and there he was, stretched out in the moonlight asleep. It must have been a dream.

Occtober 15—We are having Indian Summer weather now—almost oppressively warm. I have been wandering about all day, unable to settle down to anything. This morning I felt so lonesome that when I took the breakfast dishes down, I tried to strike up a conversation with Mrs. Harlan.

Hitherto I have found her as solemn and uncommunicative as the Sphinx, but as she took the tray from my hands, her wrinkles broke into the semblance of a smile. Positively at that moment it seemed to me that she resembled Arthur. Was it her smile, or the expression of her eyes? Has she, also, something to tell me?

"Don't you get lonesome here?" I asked her sympathetically.

She shook her head. "No, sir, I'm used to it now. I couldn't stand it anywhere else."

"And do you expect to go on living here the rest of your life?"

"That may not be very long, sir," she said, and smiled again.

Her words were simple enough, but the way she looked at me when she uttered them seemed to give them a double meaning. She hobbled away, and I went upstairs and wrote Mrs. O'Brien to expect me early on the morning of the 19th.

October 18—Ten a.m.—Am catching the twelve o'clock train tonight. Thank God, I had the resolution to get away! I believe another week of this life would drive me mad. And perhaps Arthur is right—perhaps I shall never come back.

I ask myself if I have become such a weakling as that, to desert him when he needs me most. I don't know. I don't recognize myself any longer. . . .

But of course I will be back. There is the translation, for one thing, which is coming along famously. I could never forgive myself for dropping it at the most vital point.

As for Arthur, when I return I intend to give in to him no longer. I will make myself master here and cure him against his will. Fresh air, change of scene, a good doctor, these are the things he needs.

But what is his malady? Is it the influence of this house that has fallen on him like a blight? One might imagine so, since it is having the same effect on me.

Yes, I have reached that point where I no longer sleep. At night I lie awake and try to keep my eyes off the mirror across the room. But in the end I always find myself staring into it—watching the door with the heavy bolts. I long to rise from the bed and draw back the bolts, but I'm afraid.

How slowly the day goes by! The night will never come!

* * *

Nine P.M.—Have packed my suitcases and put the room in order. Arthur must be asleep. . . . I'm afraid the parting from him will be painful. I shall leave here at eleven o'clock in order to give myself plenty of time... It is beginning to rain....

October 19—At last! It has come! I am mad! I knew it! I felt it creeping on me all the time! Have I not lived in this house a month? Have I not seen? . . . To have seen what I have seen, to have lived for a month as I have lived, one must be mad. . . .

It was ten o'clock. I was waiting impatiently for the last hour to pass. I had seated myself in a rocking-chair by the bed, my suitcases beside me, my back to the mirror. The rain no longer fell. I must have dozed off.

But all at once I was wide awake, my heart beating furiously. Something had touched me. I leapt to my feet, and, as I turned sharply, my eyes fell upon the mirror. In it I saw the door just as I had seen it the other night, and the figure fumbling with the bolt. I wheeled around, but there was nothing there.

I told myself that I was dreaming again, that Arthur was asleep in his bed. But I trembled as I opened the door of his room and peered in. The room was empty, the bed not even crumpled. Lighting a match, I groped my way through the bathroom into the library.

The moon had come from under a cloud and was pouring in a silvery flood through the windows, but Arthur was not there. I stumbled back into my room.

The moon was there, too. . . And the door, the door in the corner was half open. The bolt had been drawn. In the darkness I could just make out a flight of steps that wound upward.

I could no longer hesitate. Striking another match, I climbed the back stairway.

When I reached the top I found myself in total darkness, for the blinds were tightly closed. Realizing that the room was probably a duplicate of the one below, I felt along the wall until I came to the gas jet. For a moment the flame flickered, then burned bright and clear.

O God! what was it I saw? A table, thick with dust, and something wrapped in a reddish-brown dressing-gown, that sat with its elbows propped upon it.

How long had it been sitting there, that it had grown more dry than the dust upon the table! For how many thousands of days and nights had the flesh rotted from that grinning skull!

In its bony fingers it still clutched a pencil. In front of it lay a sheet of scratched paper, yellow with age. With trembling fingers I brushed away the dust. It was dated October 19, 1912. It read:

"Dear Tom:

"Old man, can you run down to see me for a few days? I'm afraid I'm in a bad way—"

The
Cavern

Manly Wade Wellman

Manly Wade Wellman

"The Cavern" originally appeared under the byline of Manly Wade Wellman and Gertrude Gordon. When asked about Ms. Gordon some years ago, Wellman admitted she was just a friend who wanted to see her name in print, and the story was entirely his creation. "The Cavern" plays games with the reader. It dares you to match wits with the author. Can you guess the secret of the cavern before reading the last line of the story?

The Cavern

Manly Wade Wellman

*We tread the steps appointed for us; and he
whose steps are appointed must tread them.*
—*The Arabian Nights.*

The old fortune-teller had done with her prattle about cross-
ing water and receiving letters full of money. She gathered up her
grimy deck of cards and shuffled away, leaving Stoll and me to finish our dinner under soft lights, accompanied by soft music. I
sighed and wondered aloud why the hag had singled us out of all
the patrons in the crowded restaurant.

"Because she knew I believe," replied Stoll as he poured
wine.

I was amazed and a bit shocked. "You believe in fortune-tell-
ers? Nobody of education and intelligence can possibly—"

"Granted that I have no education and intelligence, but I believe." He was quite solemn. "I've seen one come true."

I dared hope for one of Stoll's rare stories. Why do men like
Stoll, who have seen so much and behaved so well in far places,
keep their mouths shut? I waited, and eventually he added:

"It wasn't my fortune, but Swithin Quade's."

"Swithin Quade," I repeated eagerly. "The African Quade?
The one in the Sunday feature sections?"

"Right. I met him on his first day in Africa."

Swithin Quade was the sort of budding empire-builder
Kipling used to write about [began Stoll]. You know what I
mean—broad shoulders, long legs, golden-brown curls, eyes like
the April sky, close-clipped young mustache, close-clipped young
attitudes, and adventure hunger enough for all the explorers since
the launching of the Argo. His people had no money, but they
managed to educate him well, and through influential friends he'd

135

been signed up to cut his teeth on the tomb of a priest-noble of the Hyksos, up Nile a way. I was camp and digging chief on that job, under Thomason, the big Egyptology pot.

Alexandria was even more garish then than now—there was considerable tourist money, and no war scare. As soon as Quade hit the dock he wanted to see dancers, snake-charmers, mosques and all the rest of it. I took him 'round, because Thomson was busier than I and didn't know so many places. Quade and I wound up late the first afternoon in a loudish spot, with striped awnings, and mutton stew, and hashish in the coffee. A bunch of vicious-looking blacks were belting away at drums and wailing on pipes, and a very dirty and ragged old Arab sidled up to whine for *"Bakshish!"*

I warned him off with the traditional *"Mafish!"*, and tried to ignore him. But the old duffer—bent he was, and dried up like a bunch of raisins—began to plead for a chance to tell fortunes. Quade asked what it was all about, and I explained.

"Good egg," said Quade at once, his face as bright and happy as a child's behind that trim mustache. "Have him tell mine."

The walking mummy understood Quade's enthusiastic manner, if not his English, and right away set down his little tray of polished wood on the edge of our table. Then he poured sand on the tray, from an old tobacco pouch. He began to fiddle with his scrawny fingers, making little rifts and ridges and hills.

"Good egg," Quade repeated. "This blighter is just what I hoped to run into. Picturesque and all that—hurry up, old fellow!" And his smile grew wider.

But the sand diviner did not smile back. He only paddled in the sand, and stared out of ancient eyes that looked dim and foul, like pools with scum on them. Finally he mumbled something.

"What's he saying?" asked Quade, and I translated:

"Death sits waiting in a cavern. . . ."

The old bat had waited for me to pass this along. And now he added something on his own hook. "The other *effendi,"* he said, turning his dim gaze on me, "shall be witness, and will know that I have not lied."

Quade's grin faded into a frown of intense interest, and he leaned forward to look at the sand on the tray. It was all smoothed out, under those dirty claws, and in the middle was a little hole.

Funny that it should look so deep and dark, that hole; there wasn't more than a handful of sand, yet you'd think the diviner had made a pit miles deep.

I saw that Quade was suddenly repelled, and I gave the old vulture a piece of silver, a shilling I think. He bowed and blessed us, and gathered up his tray of sand and scrabbled out. Quade drank some coffee.

"I say, that was nasty," he mumbled to me. "Let's go back to the hotel, eh?"

So we went. But he found it was close and hot there, and stepped out to take a bit of a stroll by himself. Back he came in half an hour, and he looked quite drawn and stuffy.

"These swine are pulling my leg," he said angrily, and then he told me what had happened. Down in some narrow alley full of shops and booths, he had come upon another fortune-teller, a baggy old woman who spoke English. Probably he hoped to hear something conventional about a blonde wife and a journey across deep water, to take the taste of the other prophecy out of his mouth. So he stuck out his palm for her to read.

"And I swear, Stoll," he told me, "that she gave one look and then screwed up her face, and said the same thing."

"What same thng?" I asked him.

"What that filthy old Johnny with the sand said. 'Look out for the cavern,' or 'Death waits in the cavern,' or the like. See here, I jolly well don't like it."

I advised him to keep his chin up and not bother about natives. Finally he managed to make light of the business, but not very convincingly. And when we got to Cairo—Thomson had to stop there for a big row with the officials—he gave the business a third try.

It was in a cool, conventional little tea garden—run by a smart Scotswoman, who knew how a place like that would catch homesick English travelers. She had native waiters dressed like Europeans, and crumpets and all that, and a very lovely girl in a stagy gipsy costume to read the leaves in the cups. Quade wanted to test fate again.

The girl came to our table when he beckoned, and she was plainly intrigued by his grin and his curls and his youth. I think she intended to give him such a reading as would fetch him back later—maybe not for tea alone. But as she turned the cup and squinted at the tangle inside, her handsome face grew grave, and its olive faded to a parchment tint.

"You must take care," she said huskily, in accented English. "Take care of the cave—the cavern." Her eyes grew wider, and she looked at me with them. "You, sir, will see a terrible fate that is his. . . ."

"That night Quade packed his bags, and told Thomson and me that he was chucking his job.

"I'm not having any of that cavern," he said. "Three warnings are quite enough."

"What cavern?' I demanded, smiling a little.

"Cavern or underground tomb, what's the difference?"

"You can't take such prophecies seriously," put in Thomson.

Quade replied, very tritely, that there were more things in heaven and earth, and so on. "I know you chaps think I'm afraid," he added.

"Neither of us said anything like that," I replied at once.

"And no more am I afraid," he almost snapped back. "I'll stay in Africa—but in the open. Call me idiotic, or superstitious, or what you will. Better safe than sorry, is my motto."

He was as good as his word for ten years, and he thrived enormously on African danger.

Today he is a tradition, a legend even. Everybody has heard about how, in Jo'burg, he walked up on a mad Kaffir with a gun, who had even those tough Transvaal police buffaloed for the moment; the Kaffir fired twice, stirring Quade's curls with both shots, and then Quade knocked him loose from the gun with one straight dunt on the mouth. Some sort of foundation wanted to give him a medal, but he wouldn't accept. He went instead with some romantic Frenchman who tried to find the Dying-place of the Elephants—sure, people still look for it; I, for one, believe it exists. But all Quade got was a terrible dose of black-water fever. He recovered from that and complications, though eleven men out of twelve would have died.

Next he got up into West Central, and visited the Lavalii-valli. Instead of thinking that he was a missionary and eating him, they thought he was a god and worshipped him. I understand that Quade had to fight one skeptic, a big brute about seven feet tall, very skilful with the stabbing-spear. But Quade dodged the first thrust, got in close and took the spear away, and gave it back right through the fellow's lungs. That made him solider than teak with the Lavalli-valli, who love a fighter better than anything else in all the cosmos. Quade might have ruled there forever, but all he wanted was to trade for the native rubber they had. He got a whole caravan-load, and lost it to Portuguese gamblers in Benguela. Broke, he accepted an offer to help the inland Boer settlers fight off a Gangella uprising. He had more escapes than Bonnie Prince Charlie. Then he went to Ethiopia, just as the Italians pushed in. Quade took up for Haile Selassi, who dubbed him "Ras Quedu" and put him in command of a kind of a suicide division. His men—Africa's tallest and finest, as I hear—were slaughtered almost to the last one, in the fighting around Jijiga. But Quade was captured by some of Mussolini's Moslem auxiliaries. While the chiefs were arguing whether he should die as an infidel or live as a prisoner of war, Quade throttled a sentry and escaped. He fled clear through the interior, safe into British territory.

That and a thousand other things made him news. Lowell Thomas began talking about him on the radio, and W. B. Seabrook or somebody of that sort wrote a biography, *Quade the Incredible*. I daresay he'll be a solar myth before the century is out.

I cut his trail just about a year ago, on the fringe of a rain-forest somewhere in the 'tween-mountain country of Portuguese West. If we had a map I'd show you where. His boys and mine entered a little village from opposite sides. I, following in, heard, "Hullo there, Stoll! This *is* a lark!", and there was Quade. Not the curly golden boy any more, but a tough-tempered, lean-cheeked hunter. He had grown a short beard, into which the toothbrush mustache had lengthened and blended. His rosy face had been baked brown, and his was the ready way of moving and standing that comes from harsh life gladly met. The one thing that made me remember the old Swithin Quade—or, rather, the young Swithin Quade—was his bright blue eye, as happy and honest under his worn slouch hat as it had been that first afternoon in Alexandria.

When we had crushed each other's hands and slapped each other's backs almost purple, we quartered our outfits side by side, just at the gate of the village stockade. Then we went together to buy beans and manioc, and he invited me to supper at his fire. After eating we swapped yarns, and of course Quade's yarns were by far the best.

"You still remember those Alexandrian fortunes?" I asked at length.

He smiled, but nodded, and said that he had more than remembered.   He had asked fortunes from varied seers—Kaffir
witch-doctdors, Moslem marabouts, and ordinary crystal-gazers in
Cape Town and Durban. "And they've been strangely unanimous,"
he summed up. "I give you my word, that again and again there
been something about a cave, or a cavern, or just a hole. And I'm
always told that I'd best stay out."

"And have you stayed out?" I prompted

"I have that," he chuckled. "I must say that, if death waits for
me in a cavern, it has remained there.   Mine's the traditional
charmed life."

"Don't forget," I reminded, "that I'm supposed to witness
your fate in a cavern."

"I haven't forgotten, Stoll. But I'm here to hunt—hippopotami
just now. I've been too busy all these years to get one—and if you
come along tomorrow, we'll take care to stay clear of holes. Then,
when we separate in a day or so, I'll be safe again, what?"

I joined in chuckling over the conceit.

But he was dead serious on one point—staying in the open.
That night he slept in a tent, not the snug hut that the solicitious
villagers had built especially for him. His gun-bearer told my head-
man that Quade always slept that way; that, when in the settle-
ments he, Quade, never sat in a house without the windows open,
and had twice refused to take a job in the diamond country for
dislike of entering a mine. I heard all this at breakfast in the morning, and made bold to ask Quade about it when he came over to
renew his invitation to the hunt.

"My bearer's a gossipy chap, but he's telling the truth,"
Quade confessed cheerfully. "I go into precious few houses except when it's necessary, and into no cellars whatever. Now then,
what heavy rifles have you? . . . Oh, I see, Dutch guns. Two nice
weapons, those. Well, shall we start?"

Away we went, with our gun-bearers and a leash of villagers
for guides. Down valley from the camp we approached a great
tangled belt of forest, and one of the local hunters pointed to a
tunnel-like opening among the trees and bushes, that "hole in the
jungle" made by nothing but a hippo.

"I say, that looks as if it might be the cavern you and I heard
about once," said Quade, and not in a joking manner. He hesitated, but only for a moment, and then led the way in.

We traversed the leafy passasge, and I felt as jumpy as Quade. But the closest approach to danger along the entire way was an ineffably beautiful little snake, that struck at a village boy and missed. My bearer killed it with a stick he carried.

At the other end of the tunnel we came out on the banks of one of those African rivers unknown and uncharted—deep, swift, tree-walled, as dark and exotic as the one in the poem about Kubla Khan. As a matter of fact, Quade muttered a phrase from that very poem about "Alph, the sacred river," but I refrained from adding the bit about "caverns measureless to man." Meanwhile, the villagers poked into a clump of sappy-leaved bushes, and drew into view a brace of dugouts, very nicely finished and perfectly balanced. Quade and his bearer got into one of them, and I with my bearer took the other. Each of us had a pair of villagers to paddle. Together we dropped downstream.

It was I, a little ahead of Quade, who saw the hippo first.

He was floating like a water-soaked log in a little bay where the current slowed down considerably., His nostril bumps were in sight, and his ears pricked up to show that they heard us, but he kept perfectly still, hoping we'd pass him by.

My bearer snapped his fingers backward to attract Quade's attention in the rear boat, and I, sitting in the bow, set my elbow on my knee and aimed for what could see of the hippo's narrow, flat cranium. He was no farther away than the door yonder—I couldn't miss. And I was using a three-ounce explosive slug, big and heavy enough to go through a brick wall.

I couldn't miss, I say. But I did miss. No, not quite; I must have nicked an ear or grazed an eyebrow. For next instant the hippo, stung and furious, swung round in the water like a a trout, and charged.

He didn't charge me. He didn't even notice me, then or later. He tore past me in the water—perhaps it was shallow enough for him to run on the bottom—straight at Quade's boat.

I heard Quade curse in Umbundu, and his express rifle roared. Whatever the bullet did, it was not enough to stop the hippo. I, snatching my second rifle from my bearer, saw the great lump of a head dip down under the keel of Quade's boat. The hippo tossed, as a bull might toss, and the canoe with its four passengers whirled lightly upward in the air. I've seen an empty bottle tossed like that, by a careless drunkard.

The three natives, shrieking horribly, flew in all directions and splashed into the water. Quade must have been braced or otherwise held in position at the bow, for when the boat came down he was still in it. There was a great upward torrent of water, and through it I saw the bottom of the stricken canoe. The hippo, close in, bit a piece out of one thwart, as a boy nibbles gingercake. I had my second gun and was aiming. This time I wouldn't miss; but before I could touch trigger, Quade came to the surface, right in the way of my shot.

"Down! Down!" I yelled at him, and he turned his face toward me, as if mildly curious at my agitation. And then the hippo had him, in a single champing clutch of those great steam-shovel jaws. Quade screamed once, and I saw him shaken like an old glove by a bulldog.

I fired, and the hippo sank on the instant. He took Quade with him. The ripples were purple with blood—Quade's or the beast's. And we got for shore and safety. Later we tried to recover Quade's body, but we never did.

*   *   *   *   *

Stoll was silent, and sipped wine to show that his story was finished.

"But the cavern," I protested. "What about the cavern, where death was waiting for him?"

Stoll lifted his eyebrows, as a Frenchman might shrug his shoulders.

"Did you ever see a hippopotamus open its mouth—wide?"

The
Wolf-
Woman

Bassett Morgan

Bassett Morgan

Bassett Morgan was the pen-name for a woman author from New York who contributed thirteen stories to Weird Tales over a span of a little more than ten years. She was remembered primarily for a number of adventures featuring sinister Chinese villains transplanting human brains into animal bodies. However, she was capable of writing fast-paced weird fiction as well. "The Wolf-Woman" combines an unusual setting, a startling discovery, and an age-old terror into a unique mixture of adventure and horror.

The Wolf-Woman

Bassett Morgan

Beaten back by fogs and blizzards of the heights, the Stamwell party was camped in a sun-warmed valley at the base of Mount Logan, which lifts its ice-capped head in eternal solitude and awful silence above the most intensely glaciated region of the world.

Three years before, in an attempt to follow MacCarthy, who first ascended Logan, the intrepid mountain-climber Morsey had fallen into a crevasse; and Professor Stamwell was now attempting to recover his body from the glacier and by a process of his own experimentation restore it to life.

His assistant, Lieutenant Cressey, who had been more intrigued by the adventure of the climb than by Stamwell's sanguinary hope of resuscitating flesh entombed and even perfectly preserved in the ice, was reluctant to admit failure. Nevertheless, he enjoyed the sun-warmth of the valley after the terrific frost-fangs and ice-claws of the heights. Along the shores of a little river whose source lay in the glaciers, the dogs romped, catching fish with the dexterity of the husky breed and gorging themselves.

Baptiste, the big half-breed Canadian guide who looked after the comforts of the men, had been roving all day. At supper time he returned, tossing his cap in the air and yelling excitedly.

"M'sieus," he shouted, "I have find wan funny mans what makes t'ings of ivory. You come an' see. You lak heem ver' much."

Nothing loth to leave the discussion of their defeat, Stamwell and Cressey followed the exuberant Baptiste for a mile or two along the river to a stoutly timbered cabin beside which an old man watched his supper cooking over a fire outside. At sight of him, Cressey laughed, while Baptiste explained his new acquaintance.

145

"Hees name ees Jo. He ees half Indian, half Eskimo. An' I savvy hees talk ver' fine."

While Baptiste talked in tribal jargon, Cressey's amusement mounted. The old man was toothless and wrinkled. A beaded band kept the lank hair from obscuring his sight, and as his jaw wagged constantly on a quid of chewing tobacco, two knobbed knucklebones of seals thrust through slits in his cheeks gave the appearance of tusks. Ragged wolf-skin trousers and elk-hide moccasins completed his attire, and he smiled grotesquely as he led the way inside the cabin. There he lighted a wick floating on a dish of oil, threw wide a window-shutter and let in sunlight, which revealed a collection of carved ivory objects on shelves about the walls.

Baptiste was even more eager than the carver to display his skill. He handed Stamwell a figure copied from comic supplements of newspapers and familiar in homes from the arctic circle to the Florida Keys. A moment later he brought forth its mate. Stamwell held in his hands cleverly chiseled likenesses of Mutt and Jeff. Flattered by the interest of these white men, Jo showed them the source of his inspiration, a sheaf of old newspapers from the pages of which he took his ivory models. Baptiste, convulsed with mirth, laid in Cressey's hand a figure which brought a responsive laugh.

"She got bellyache!" he shouted. Even Professor Stamwell chuckled at his description of a lovely little "September Morn."

They spent a good deal of time with the contents of the shelf before Jo took up the oil dish and threw a flickering light on a recumbent figure in the cabin corner. Stamwell went on his knees, and Cressey gasped at the beauty of a woman, carved in ivory, lying as if asleep with one arm under her head and her long hair draped over her shoulder. The figure was almost life-size, and the ivory block showed no seam or joint. Stamwell touched the slender leg with gentle fingers, then looked at Cressey.

"Cressey, this ivory is of different texture from the small figures. I should say it was fossilized, but where on earth would the old fellow obtain such a huge block of material?"

"And the woman-model!" exclaimed Cressey. "A white woman, undoubtedly. Look at the sensitive nostrils and straight nose, and the rounded cheeks. No Kogmollye or Indian squaw posed for this. The old fellow didn't create her, either. He couldn't. You can see he has only a great skill in imitating and copying. Baptiste, ask Jo where he saw such a woman, asleep."

Baptiste's conversation with the old man occupied some time, and before it ended the big guide was fingering his scapular.

"Jo, he say dees woman froze een ice. He git dees big chunk ivory from ver' beeg land-whale, also froze een ice."

"A land-whale! Cressey, he means a mammoth. We've come across real treasure. Baptiste, tell Jo we would like to see this land-whale."

Baptiste interpreted. The ivory-carver nodded good-naturedly and started at once to lead them to the source of his art-material.

"Jo, he say," offered Baptiste when the dogs were harnessed and food on the sled in case of an overnight trip, "he say dees womans ees froze een ice long tam. Maybe dis summer fetch her out. She come down ver' fast. Long tam ago, Jo see her ver' high up. Jo say more as hunderd snows when he first see her."

"Frozen in the glacier more than a hundred years ago! Preposterous! The old fellow exaggerates! Stamwell waved aside Jo's veracity. "We've evidently stumbled on a tragedy. Snow madness makes its victims strip naked, usually, which would account for her nudity, and Jo looks aged, but I don't credit his hundred-year memory."

"Her hair must have touched the ground, Professor. That dates her pretty far back."

For some hours the ice-trail, steep though not perilous, claimed their attention. The sun swung down to the horizon for the brief moments of northern midnight, then began its upward arc. They found that Jo had cut steps on the glacial river which wound down from the grim sides of Mount Logan. Mounting steadily, they reached a terrace which led to lofty pinnacles of ice so clearly blue it was like a fairy palace, where steps led to an outstanding archway and natural grotto of rock that had been broken from its base and carried down.

Inside the grotto the light was weirdly blue, the ice underfoot clear as glass. Jo pointed and Cressey knelt, and a moment later his cry echoed from the grotto walls. Under the crystal shell lay the carver's model, more beautiful than the carved ivory, a woman, young, lovely, golden hair half robing her form, tawny eyelashes on her rounded cheeks. Near by, as if they had lain down to sleep and been caught by instant and painless death, were seven large hounds or wolves, with snow-white pelts.

Baptiste, plagued by superstitious fear, gazed long and earnestly, then leaped from the cave with a wild cry and ran down the steps which led to the broken end of the lower terrace. Cressey and Stamwell, engrossed by the sight beneath their feet, did not miss Baptiste until he returned, holding his nose and grimacing.

"Name of a Name! She smell ver' dead, dat land-whale!"

They followed him to the terrace, below which lay the enormous carcass of a hairy mammoth in advanced stages of putrefaction, smelling, as Baptiste had said, "very dead."

One great tusk lay on the tundra, the other had been sawn off, proving Jo's assertion about the source of his ivory. Cressey was staring at the mass below in absorbed silence, when Stamwell clutched his arm and exclaimed: "Cressey, we did not find Morsey. But we've found this woman. By heaven, we'll take her and her dogs from their ice-tomb!"

"But—but what a pity!" cried Cressey. "The air will finish them in no time, like that mammoth. She is beautiful in death!"

"Another summer would bring her down to that finish anyway," argued Stamwell. "And what if it isn't death? What about its being merely suspended animation? Here is our chance to test my discovery. I meant to try it on Morsey. We can't do that for him, but what a triumph to bring this woman back to life after God alone knows how many years of sleep; a Diana of eld and her hunting pack!"

"But aren't you interested in this mammoth at all, Stamwell?"

"What is a mammoth, decayed at that?" Stamnwell's eyes burned with the passion of a zealot. "Mammoths have been found everywhere, their skeletons mounted and their existence traced. We shouldn't have even the satisfaction of originality. But to carry out a living woman who has been buried in the ice, no one can say how long—Cressey, look at those hounds!" Stamwell was hurrying to the cave and growing more excited every moment. "Do you know of a living breed of dogs like them? They are true wolf, even larger than the timber wolves. And albinos. It is stupendous, staggering, the antiquity revealed under this shell of ice. And to think, if we had been a year later this superb discovery would have moved down with the glacier and broken off at the terrace, the prey of wild animals, the bones scattered. That will happen next year unless we rescue her!"

Cressey did not answer. The idea of taking this frozen beauty from the ice and restoring her to life sounded like the talk of a man demented. Yet, as he heard the calculating plan of Stamwell unfold, Cressey admitted to himself that it was a new and alluring adventure. At Stamwell's succinct commands, he accompanied Baptiste to the valley camp to bring back their packs and establish a camp in the grotto which penetrated the floe for a hundred feet or more and would serve admirably as a shelter.

By the time Baptiste had made beds of pine boughs and started a fire with wood hauled from below, Cressey found that Stamwell had made remarkable progress in chipping the ice from the entombed woman and her dogs. The guide cooked breakfast. The cave had assumed an appearance of comfort exceeding their valley tents, and after a meal of flapjacks they slept.

Cressey was wakened by the noise of Stamwell's pick on the ice.

"What if that hammering should start an avalanche?" he asked.

"There isn't much danger. The sun warmth melting the ice also welds it, and the floe is less crisp here than in higher altitudes. Don't think up discouragements, Cressey. Get busy and help me."

They worked all day, cutting a rectangular space which included the entire group. Baptiste and the other half-breeds had slept huddled in parkas, in the tents erected outside the grotto, which they refused to enter except to carry out the broken ice. It was apparent to both Stamwell and Cressey that their men regarded this disturbance of the ice-entombed woman as a sacrilege that would brew trouble, and Baptiste solemnly voiced prophetic warning.

"Dogs!" he snorted. "Who ever see dogs lak dem? Dey look more lak ghost-wolf, the *loup-garou*. Me, I don' lak dees bisniss. I come for to climb mountain, not dig up dead womans." Nor would he gaze into the deepening hole where Stamwell and Cressey labored until only a thin shell of ice covered the bodies of the woman and hounds, when Stamwell called a halt.

"We must prepare things for her resuscitation, Cressey. Help me with these packs."

They toiled until Cressey reeled with weariness, preparing ice slabs covered with furs, arranging apparatus, pulmonary respirators, hypodermics, bottles of precious distillations known only to Professor Stamwell, blankets and kettles of hot water.

"If you should be tempted to give an account of this to the world, Cressey, I trust you will guard the secret of my process," said Stamwell that night.

"Obviously," answered Cressey, "since I haven't the faintest idea of success in such a preposterous attempt to cheat death."

Buoyed up by excitement, Stamwell seemed unwearied, but Cressey was glad to lie down, and it seemed only a few moments of sleep when again he was awakened by Stamwell's chipping ice in the task of extricating one of the white hounds. By noontime, they were lifting it from the hole and placing it on a fur-covered slab of ice to be rolled in blankets and be gradually warmed with hot water cans until the nine-inch length of fur fell wet and limp as it thawed.

It was some time before the flesh grew pliable, for the beast measured eleven feet from snout to tail-tip and was all the two men could manage. With sweat pouring down his face, Cressey obeyed the crisp commands of Stamwell with trained military precision while the professor applied one after another of his processes and both took turns in expanding and contracting the great fur-clad chest by sheer strength, and manipulating the hypodermic of fluid which started heart action. Then Cressey felt a twitching of the body muscles and saw the legs jerk. He could scarcely credit his sight as Stamwell poured small doses of prepared broth down the dog's throat, and it swallowed them with a faint, gurgling whimper. Stamwell's cry held triumph.

In vain Baptiste announced mealtime. The sun had dipped and begun another day before the great hound was swathed in blankets and furs and the two white men took the hot coffee they sorely needed.

"Eureka!" shouted Stamwell, beside himself with joy.

"And now that the beast is alive, what will we do with him?" was Cressey's rejoinder.

"Take excellent care of him. Take him down to the valley as soon as possible, where Baptiste can feed and look after him."

After a brief three hours of sleep, Stamwell roused Cressey and they exhumed another hound, going through the same laborious work as before, to be rewarded eventually by a whimpering whine and the signs of recurring animation. By that time the first hound was able to take boiled meat and showed ravenous greed, and after the meal it attempted to struggle to its feet but was still weak. In three days it left the blankets and took a few staggering steps, then lifted its magnificent head and howled mournfully again and again, a sound at which Baptiste made the sign of the cross and muttered Chippewan incantations against evil.

When ten days were gone, Baptiste was delegated to escort a pack of seven white hounds, for which stout leather collars and light chains were provided, to the valley. With him went all the half-breeds except one who remained to cook for the white men in the grotto. Baptiste had orders to hunt game and feed the hounds and keep the sled dogs on leash at the cabin of the ivory-carver for greater safety.

With the grotto cleared of the dogs, Stamwell turned his attention to the central block of ice. The hypodermic needles were carefully sterilized, and the greatest care and precautions taken as they lifted the crystal casket from the hole and carefully thawed the ice embedding the woman. Sweat poured off both men while they worked, and their breaths came in sharp hisses long before the first sign of life was evinced in a whispered sigh from the pale lips.

Stamwell's eyes were shadowed to the cheekbones and he seemed to have aged years when the muscular twitching of her slender legs began and a sigh of agony quivered into the silence.

"If you've had your flesh frozen and thawed, you will understand the pain she feels," said Stamwell. "I almost regret inflicting this suffering upon her, but when she pulls through and realizes that she is alive, then, Cressey, I shall be repaid."

Cressey's thoughts denied that potential gratitude. Suppose this woman had been dead any great length of time and found none of her own generation alive in the world, would she thank them? Cressey doubted it, but she was so lovely that he lost all sense of dread and felt only a vast pity in his heart for the beautiful creature lying in the red blankets, her golden hair spread like a silken veil on the colored wool.

It was almost midnight when her eyelids fluttered open and the two men saw eyes of purple softness which moved slowly as she seemed aware of the two men and the firelight illuminating the dark ice of the cave. The blueness left her fingernails and color returned to her lips as she was fed hot milk and broth; then her eyelids closed and her body relaxed in sleep. Stamwell was like a man insane with fear until he applied a stethoscope to her breast.

"Thank God, it is sleep!" he cried. "But there will be no peace for me until she is out of danger. While I watch her, you had better rest. Cressey, do you realize that I have brought the dead to life?"

To Cressey his cry was a challenge, a sacrilege. He felt something of the same uncanny fear which Baptitste had displayed at Stamwell's assumption of supernatural power, and wondered if it were beneficence or crime to restore that lovely creature to life after her long sleep.

His sleep was troubled because in the valley the great hounds howled all night. Dozing, waking to curse them, he saw Stamwell beside the woman's couch, and rising he bade the professor sleep while he watched. He made coffee and carried a steaming cup to his seat beside the sleeping beauty, sipping it as he gazed at the sun-gold creeping down the glacier to the grotto door. A sigh roused him. A white hand touched his wrist. Turning, Cressey was aware the the violet eyes of the woman gazed at him and she smiled, then her fingers touched the tin cup he held as if she was thirsty.

"I can't give you that," he found himself telling her as if she understood his talk. He reached for a bowl of broth simmering on the alcohol stove, heavy with meat juices and nourishing tonic medicines, and fed her. Color tinted her throat and cheeks. She seemed momentarily to gain strength. Cressey was thrilled and awed by the miracle happening before his eyes, and shocked at the languorous coquetry of her glance and the white fingers clinging to his hand.

Again he fed her, aware that she was ravenously hungry, until the broth was finished. He thought she was again asleep until her hand lifted her golden hair and trailed it across his face and a low-toned, throaty laugh startled him. Feeling helpless in face of a crisis, he replaced the golden tress on the couch and felt his fingers tingling as from a light galvanic shock at its touch. He leaned forward and instantly his neck was circled by her arms and she pressed her face against his throat. Cressey was so astonished that he did not try to draw back, and an instant later he felt her teeth on the flesh of his neck.

Alarm and swift revulsion seized him. He was afraid to tear her arms away for fear of bruising the tender skin. He knew her heart beat under the forced stimulation of Stamwell's drugs and feared a sudden shock might halt its action, then while he hesitated a strange drowsiness clouded his senses and stole over his body. He felt no pain where her teeth pierced the skin of his throat; her arms were satin-smooth, the warmth of her lips tempted him to rest in the alluring embrace.

Then a cry from Stamwell roused Cressey from drowsiness that nearly swung into blissful unconsciousness. He was wrenched from her arms and felt the sting of flesh her teeth released. Glancing at her, he saw her lips moist and crimson-stained, and she was struggling in the clutch of Stamwell.

"Fill that hypo with the medicine in the third bottle, quickly, Cressey. She is so strong I can scarcely control her."

Cressey obeyed, even to inserting the needle into the skin of her arm. Her scream was piercing as she fought Stamwell, who held her until the drug took effect and she sank back, relaxed. Then Stamwell turned to Cressey.

"Good God, man, I trusted you to stay awake and watch."

Cressey did not reply. Stamwell was disinfecting the wound on his neck, to which he applied a pad of cotton gauze and adhesive tape. Cressey could not even smile, nor would he tell Stamwell how she had coquetted with him before catching him in her arms.

A few minutes later they saw Baptiste toiling up the glacial drift, and from outside the grotto door he called to them.

"*M'sieus,* I can not hold dose dog, dey grow so beeg, so strong, an' my men ees scare' dey break dem chain. I am ver' scare' of dose dog my own self. Me, I am good dog-man, but not dat kind of dog. I feed heem nineteen rabbit, seven coyote, wan elk and much fish in wan week. All my men do ees hunt for feed dose dog. Me, I am 'bout ready quit my job. I tak sled dogs an' tie heem across rivaire cause eef dose white dog git loose—well, we walk back outside."

"Cressey, the white hounds must not kill our sled dogs and Baptiste must be pacified, for if he deserted we should never get our menagerie out alive. I think we can take the woman down to the valley by tomorrow. Suppose you go down now and look after the camp."

Following Baptiste down the ice-trail, Cressey saw the ivory-carver industriously sawing off the remaining tusk of the mammoth, and watching him for a moment, he slipped and fell headlong. He was only slightly stunned, but a worse calamity had befallen, for in extricating his foot from a small fissure, he felt the snapping of bone and a dull pain. Cressey cursed.

"Baptiste, I've snapped a bone!" The warm-hearted Baptiste lifted him to his shoulder and made his way down to the valley, where their arrival started a terrific din of howling dogs and answering yelps of the sled huskies leashed across the river. Baptiste muttered oaths.

"Eef dose white dog git loose, dey swallow my dog lak I swallow loche-liver without chew heem," he commented and grumbled his distaste of the whole business of the grotto miracle. Baptiste was about ready to desert, and it occurred to Cressey that he had better summon Stamwell at once. The great white hounds leaped the length of their chains and the sturdy pine trees were swaying and jerking from the lunge of their powerful bodies.

"Baptiste, you had better fetch Professor Stamwell and his packs down at once, and we'll make a start outside," he said. Again Baptiste took the trail to the grotto, while Cressey soaked his foot in hot water, then bound it with wet moss and cotton. The cook was preparing supper, the other men had gone to assist old Jo to fetch his mammoth tusk to his cabin, then they all came to where Cressey sat and one of the breeds translated Jo's talk.

"M'sieu, he say eet ees not good to stay where devils come to life. Dees white wolf ees devil-wolf. Dis woman ees devil-woman. Jo, he say we better froze de dogs and womans again and go out, queeck."

"He's a timid, superstitious old man," said Cressey. "The dogs are savage but the woman can not harm anyone."

Yet as he spoke Cressey felt uneasy. The gauze pad on his neck was a reminder of his personal experience with the woman. He ate supper and waited impatiently for the coming of Stamwell, but it was nearly midnight when he saw Baptiste coming down swiftly, alone. The big guide broke into excited cries as he ran toward Cressey.

"M'sieu! Le professeur ees dead, an' *la femme,* she ees gone!"

"Gone! Stamwell dead!" echoed Cressey. Baptiste crossed himself and muttered broken snatches of Chippewan mingled with Roman Catholic prayers, looking apprehensively at the hounds. The dogs stood silent but alert, ears stiffly pointed, and sniffing the wind.

"M'sieu, een de cave ev'thing toss dees way and dat. *Le professeur* he ees lay on floor and hees t'roat ees got bite. Hees hands dey look lak dey soak in water long tam."

Like a blow from a bludgeon the explanation crashed on Cressey. When Stamwell dozed, the woman had caught him as she seized Cressey, possibly drained his blood like vampire bats of southern caves, and with renewed strength had left the grotto. He remembered that she was unclad and the air of the ice-fields bitterly cold. With his injured foot he was hampered in reaching the glacier, and nothing he could say or do would persuade Baptiste and his men to search and bring the woman to the valley.

Stamwell's death had come so suddenly he could not yet realize the tragedy. Then he noticed that the dogs were rousing to uncanny excitement, whining and growling, tugging strenuously at their chains. Cressey began to regret bitterly what had been done and longed to break camp and escape from the weird influences loosed by Stamwell and himself. Baptiste saw him look toward the ivory-carver's cabin.

"Good, *M'sieu*. We camp tonight een Jo's house. Eet ees not good to be here. *Non!*"

Under Baptiste's commands the men toiled to carry everything to the cabin, then they set about strengthening it with a barricade of young firs quickly cut down and heaped about the log walls.

"The good priest, he say all trees ees made by *le bon Dieu*," explained Baptiste, "an', Name of a Name! we need Heem dis night to keep us safe." Cressey could only nod assent, for as he dropped on a couch of freshly cut pine branches, he was aware that stealing over him was that same blissful unrest he had felt in the arms of the death-delivered woman of the glacier. He felt possessed of a wild desire to find her and thrill again to the touch of her satin arms and her mouth warm on his flesh. He knew it for an evil thing, a worse craving than whisky or dope, and found himself battling the weakness of flesh with arguments prompted by reason which his lips betrayed to Baptiste.

"It is cruel to let the woman wander alone on the ice. If you do not go and find her, Baptiste, I will."

The breed's dark face was grim with dogged determination.

"*M'sieu,* you do not leave dis cabin, not eef we must chain you lak wan dog. Me, I t'ink you have evil curse on you!"

And Baptiste barred both door and window of the cabin which held eight men, until within an hour of midnight the air had grown hot and foul and Cressey demanded fresh air. Reluctantly, Batpiste threw open the window-shutter and admitted a bar of diminishing sunlight. The white hounds were giving tongue in unearthly howling, mournful as dog-wailings which to the superstitious folk announce death, and the blood of Cressey was leaping as at the cry of a hunting pack. He hobbled to the window and looked toward the glacier where Stamwell lay. Even now he could scarcely realize that his friend was dead, and again he urged Baptiste to open the door.

"No, for my life, *M'sieu*. Look!" There in the river of slow-moving ice stood the huntress, poised daintily on her toes as if in a dance, her arms uplifted to cup her hands at her lips, her long golden hair blowing about a body as softly rounded as a young girl. And on the midnight silence came a clear, ringing cry.

Instantly pandemonium broke loose among the white hounds. Their howls were deafening and the clank of chains made wild, metallic music, and they leaped, and fell back, and leaped again. With their heads thrust through the window opening, Baptiste and Cressey watched, leaning back against men crowded behind them, as one of the hounds snapped his chain and raced like a white cloud in great, swift bounds toward the glacier.

Within a few moments they were all free and flying to the heights, where they leaped about the woman with joyous yelps until she was hidden by a frenzied tumult of gigantic hounds. Then, seemingly at her command, their yelps ceased and they were squatted on their haunches at her feet, pink eyes shining like rubies in the soft twilight, red tongues lolling and quivering from white-fanged jaws. Again she cupped hands to her lips and sent out her hunting cry. At the sound, Cressey shivered. In every nerve he felt the piercing lure of that wail. She was calling him forth, and some hell-born desire to answer and go to her was fighting every prompting of reason. Again came her call, and Cressey plunged from the window toward the door. But Baptiste was too quick for him and thrust his own great bulk against the timbers, flinging Cressey aside.

"*Non! M'sieu,* are you crazee? Look!" Baptiste had snatched a small silver crucifix from inside his shirt and clamped it against Cressey's forehead. He felt it searing his skin, like white-hot metal, and he sank to the pine couch, shuddering, sweat breaking out on his face. At Baptiste's command the men held Cressey down, and again Baptiste flattened the crucifix over his breast and repeated bits of prayers strangely mixed with the incantations of his Chippewan mother's teaching. The sweat grew clammy on his body before Baptiste released him and gave him whisky from an emergency flask.

A somber group of men waited in the cabin until the sun was sailing high and the last faint howling of the white hounds had dwindled to silence. Cressey slept and wakened to see the door open and feel the warm wind blowing through the cabin, then Baptiste brought him coffee and flapjacks hot from the pan.

"*M'sieu,* I say to Jo that we use wan sled to carry out hees beeg tusk. We have sled to spare now we don' carry out medicine packs. Today we break camp."

Cressey considered in silence, his mind quite clear, the horror of the night-frenzy vanished with the sunlight. He could not, would not go outside and leave Stamwell's body without decent burial and said so.

"*M'sieu,* what happen hees body makes no nev' mind. Me, Baptiste, say you do not go to dat cave no more. Eet ees *la Chasse du Diable!*'

"Call it what you will, Baptiste. I do not leave here without placing the body of my friend out of reach of wolves. Perhaps already the white hounds have found it. If so, I shall be haunted for life."

"Me, I t'ink dat ees happen already, *M'sieu,*" commented Baptiste, "but now dey are gone, maybe we go fetch down *le professeur.*" Baptiste had clashed wills with Cressey before, and met defeat, yet when they dragged Cressey up the ice-trail on a sled the breed wore crucifix and scapular in full view on his breast and every man did likewise.

They found no trace of the hounds, not even pad-marks on the snow. The grotto showed signs of a struggle, but fortunately Stamwell had packed his medicines and instruments. His body lay on the couch, relaxed before rigor mortis set in, and his face had even the semblance of a smile, but on his throat was an ominous white mark of strong, even teeth, and the visible skin was puckered as if his veins were empty. Otherwise the corpse was unmolested, at which Cressey marveled until he remembered that the white hounds had been supplied with meat by the men. The gaping ice-hole presented a solution of a temporary tomb, and Professor Stamwell, blanket-wrapped, was laid deep, the broken ice shoveled in, and heated water poured until the grave was filled and already freezing, safe against depredation.

It was while that task engrossed him that Cressey felt the force of the tragedy and a growing desire to avenge the murder of Stamwell, and he forgot the weird spell of the night in which the un-tombed woman had tempted him to follow her by the memory of her beauty and blissful languor of her caress. Then he remembered that since the conquest of Mount Logan by MacCarthy, other parties had set out, and he knew approximately the location of three groups headed for that ascent, all hard-headed mountain-climbers and scientists. Giving orders to Baptiste to dispatch men in search of these expedition-groups, he started up the glacier in spite of the vehement protests of the guide, who, just before leaving on the valley trail, tossed over Cressey's head the deerskin thong holding the crucifix.

"Wan ver' good priest bless it, *M'sieu*. You take care of heem for Baptiste."

Irreligious himself, Cressey respected the faiths of other men and humored Baptiste. Then, drawn on a sled by two breeds, he adventured the heights, watching for a glimpse of the woman.

They had traversed a considerable distance, had seen ptarmigan tame as chickens, and edelweiss growing through the snow. Halting to pluck one of these brave little blooms, Cressey saw something glittering over a flower that seemed withered in first unfolding, and he picked from it a long, glistening thread of gold hair that curled, by some attraction of warm blood, about his fingers.

The snow-glare was blinding, the wind whistled keen as whip-lashes, and to eat their meal sheltered from its cutting blast, Cressey ordered a detour toward a group of ice-spires which on closer inspection proved a labyrinthine entrance of shining columns leading to a second grotto. Leaning on a stout fir branch used as a cane, he limped down the passage, then halted in alarm. Low, menacing growls and clanking metal told of the hounds within, and a moment later they had leaped forth, a cloud of white death!

Cressey turned to run, knowing how meager was his chance for life. His revolver was in his hand, but as shots rang out, the hounds circled past him, apparently untouched, while he reeled in shocked amazement that he had missed a hit at such close range. Screams from the ice entrance brought his heart to his throat, cries of the two breeds that were drowned in the bay of wolves on the kill. Cressey stood paralyzed, unable to prevent the dreadful carnage, unable to save his men even while he pumped lead into that swirling, milling cloud of destruction now fighting fiercely over the mangled remains of their victims.

Weakly, he leaned against the ice wall, his senses reeling as he reloaded his revolver with trembling fingers, knowing lead was impotent against these ghost-wolves. For he knew them, now, to be more than flesh and blood. They were some infernal incarnation invulnerable to man-dealt destruction.

A high-pitched, ringing call, clear as a bugle, brought his gaze to the grotto and he saw the woman standing against the blue gloom, golden hair wind-blown, poised on her toes. She glided, dazzlingly lovely, toward him with arms outstretched, and in his last moment of reason Cressey threw one wrist up to shield his eyes from that dread allure. Then again he felt the fierce desire of her and flung out his arms. She came within five feet of him and halted, a puzzled expression on her features, her hands sweeping and weaving as if she tried to tear from between them some barrier invisible to Cressey. When he tried to seize her, she retreated, still fighting at the space separating them until man and woman reached the entrance to the ice passage, where the dogs leaped back from too close a contact, and with a gesture of despair she turned and ran, calling in her ringing voice and leading her pack to the heights. Cressey fell on his knees beside the gnawed bones of his men and heard his own cries imploring her to return.

Sweat rained from his face, his body quivered; he was a man corroded by the poison of an evil desire. After a long time his head lifted and he clutched at the crucifix on his breast, then reason gradually conquered and as he pressed it to his lips he felt the sun-warmth and cool wind and knew he was himself. Slowly, painfully, he retraced his trail down the glacier and found Baptiste had reached the lower grotto and was searching for him, frantic with fear.

"The two men are dead, eaten by the white hounds," he told Baptiste, and shuddered at the breed's cry of horror. "Take me down and bind me in the cabin, Baptiste. I am a man accursed."

"Help will come wit' dose men I send out, *M'sieu,*" comforted Baptiste.

But they waited for three days, seeing nothing of the white hounds and woman, until one man returned, a trapper old on the trails, and with chattering teeth told a tale of horror.

"White wolves broke into the first camp I git to, *M'sieu,* and I find only wan man alive. He tell me of *La Chasse du Diable,* then he die. *M'sieu,* I am ver' old man. But I hear when I was babee, of this *Chasse du Diable,* from my gran'-gran'-pere, an' hees gran'-pere tell heem."

For a week they waited the return of the second man sent out, then one morning Baptiste reported men coming up the valley, and Cressey hobbled to meet them.

"Thank God you've come!" he cried. "My name is Cressey. My companion, Professor Stamwell, is dead, and I have a tale to tell almost beyond belief."

"I'm Johnson," said the leader of the newcomers, "and I think I know something of your story. Your man told us a little and we found the Stillwell camp ravaged—a terrible sight. I'm worried about another party toward the west, for we had a friendly wager as to who would first climb Logan. But I am amazed at the hunger of wolves in summer, that they attack men."

"These are more than wolves, Johnson, as Baptiste will tell you." Cressey began to relate his adventures, omitting nothing, not even his own accursed desire which had recurred each night and which Baptiste fought with incantation and holy symbol.

"Laugh if you will. To me it is horrible," he ended.

"I'm not even smiling. Your face shows the strain, Cressey. But have you nerve enough to accompany me and the men to the grotto again?"

"Of course. Waiting here is hell."

Johnson and Baptiste held weighty consultations while Cressey lay on the grass, too pain-wracked to take part. His lips twisted in a sneer when the men made rude crosses of wood and gathered a blanket full of windflowers, those pale blooms which Indian converts say "spring up where angels' tears have fallen," and loaded sleds. Cressey was oblivious to everything but the fact that he was returning to the grotto where he had seen the Huntress, and with a low cunning that shamed him he was plotting a meeting with her that should cradle him in her arms.

They threaded the passageway of ice turrets, carrying pine torches which gave smoky light to the blueness of the grotto as Johnson examined it, then flung himself on the ice floor with a cry.

"Cressey, for God's sake, look! Here's a mammoth, as I'm alive. And other beasts. Lord, man, some mighty convulsion of nature must have herded your huntress, her wolves, and other denizens of her long-departed era into close quarters and caught them. Good heavens, if your secret process will restore the woman and wolves, why not try it on bigger game?"

Cressey laughed. The evil spell of the place had caught Johnson, and if he could be persuaded to carry out this wild scheme of digging up this frozen mammoth, there would be time . . . time to seek again his Huntress and find the Lethe of her embrace.

Through ensuing talk, Cressey was enthusiastic. The men were sent to bring the packs from the first grotto, and the digging began. About the cave entrance, the wooden crosses were arranged with arms touching and draped with windflowers that were also scattered on the ice trail. Cressey's own men and Baptiste refused to assist the ice-digging. Jo, the ivory-carver, was still below in his cabin. Nothing would persuade him to take part.

"Old Jo declares this woman and her dogs are evil, yet he seems unafraid," Cressey remarked one day.

"Jo," interrupted Baptiste, "he say he too old, an' have not much blood. He say he make charm een hees ivory womans. When dis hunter-womans come, he pick up ax and smash ivory womans, an' the ghost-womans go 'way and nev' come back."

"Oddly enough, the natives of the south seas and Africa have the same belief," said Johnson. "They make an image of some enemy and either burn it or put it in water to rot, and the object of their venom sickens and dies. The world, Cressey, is small."

That night, as the sun sank lower, came the howling of wolves, and Cressey felt the prickling of his scalp and leap of blood. Although toil-weary, the men were awake, and guns in hand they watched the great white hounds streaking down the glacier, led by the flying huntress. Cressey started for the ice-passage, but Baptiste leaped and bore him down, his great weight pressing the breath from the smaller man as he struggled and fought in sudden rage. Subsiding, he laughed, but the sound of his laughter was unpleasant even to his own hearing.

It seemed as if the party had small chance of defense against those ghastly, ravening death-wolves, but to the amazement of every man, the pack halted abruptly beyond the wooden crosses, and the huntress stood there twisting her hands as if baffled. The crosses and blessed windflowers had turned the hunt, but there began hours of fearful waiting until the pack circled the pinnacles, even leaping over the grotto arch and howling from behind the fence of crosses over the cave entrance. The sun was well above the horizon when they drifted away.

Night after night the diabolic chase returned only to retreat, baffled by barriers they could not break down. By day the men slaved to unearth the frozen beast belonging to an era when the north was tropic swale. Baptiste, who hunted in the valley for fresh meat, reported that Jo was carving a second figure of the huntress, standing upright, extremely lifelike, and that he scarcely left his work to eat or sleep.

At last the great hairy mammoth lay clear of ice, and because they had no means of lifting its immense weight from the hole, Cressey and Johnson built fires about it, shielded from the carcass by screens of flattened oil-cans until it was thawed and restoratives from Stamwell's stores applied. Blankets and fur robes were shoved under it by leverage of cut pine sticks, and all hands rubbed the gigantic limbs and trunk with rough pads of twigs bound together by coarse grass. It was a Herculean task and the men were exhausted before the monster shuddered, stirred his mighty body, strained ponderously while everyone scrambled out of the ice-hole. Then, heaving himself to his knees, the mammoth staggered slowly to his feet. As the puny humans fled from his path, he crushed the ice under his forefeet, burst the ropes with which he had been bound, and lumbered out of his tomb, his tusks crashing down the ice-pinnacles of the passage and scattering the protecting crosses. Then he lunged to the glacial river and went tottering to the valley.

Cressey, white-faced and shaking as he realized the titanic grimness of the thing he and Johnson had loosed, ordered the trek to begin immediately down the ice-floe to the valley. At the same time he realized that, working with pick and shovel, concentrating on the healthful task of manual labor, he had liberated his mind and body from the huntress' evil sway. He no longer paid attention to the midnight *Chasse du Diable,* and he slept soundly through the baying of ghost-wolves. He breathed deep drafts of the balsam-laden valley warmth as they approached Jo's cabin, reverently thankful for his release.

"Baptiste," he said gently, "you have looked after me and I am grateful. I have been caught in the power of hell, but it is gone."

Baptiste caught him by the arms and looked deep into his eyes.

"*Oui, M'sieu.* No more I can see dat woman-shape in your eyeball. All dees time, eet was dere an' I know you are een her power. Now, eet ees gone!"

Cressey felt a tremor of apprehension. He had not known that the image of the huntress was photographed on the retinas of his eyes until Baptiste spoke of it. He held out his hand and the breed gripped it in a solemnity of silence that was like prayer, then he pointed to the almost finished figure at which Jo worked assiduously, never lifting his hands from the task. The delicacy of his skill was never so apparent as now. From the the ivory base still shrouding her feet, the huntress seemed to dance, wind-blown hair, curving limbs, round young breasts so perfect that it seemed a pity he could not, like Pygmalion of old, breathe life into this Galatea. Cressey put out a hand to touch it but Jo waved him aside and yelped a warning.

"He say you mus' not touch her, or you have devil in your liver some more," translated Baptiste.

"Tell him I shall buy her and pay well," said Cressey, but Baptiste returned a disconcerting negative.

"Jo say, he keep her for to lay curse you have loos' een dees world. Now, *M'sieu,* we go outside."

But this time it was Jo who demurred at departure. His harangue, interpreted by Baptiste, told Cressey that he was responsible for releasing the powers of darkness in the valley and it was no longer safe to be caught on the trail at night until the evil was overcome. This simple acceptance by the old ivory-carver of the presence of terrifying supernatural powers did more to persuade Johnson than all Cressey's talk.

"They're merely flesh and blood animals," he argued. "We may have to take precautions as we would with any wild beasts, but I mean to follow that mammoth and herd him into some museum."

In the sun-warmed valley, where fires and cooking spread the comfort of commonplace occurrences, it was easier to lay aside superstitious fears, and when Baptiste's convictions were strengthened by Jo's calm acceptance of peril, Cressey realized he would better bow to their opinion that they take the river instead of land trails on the way out, and for this purpose Baptiste was already cutting timber to make rafts, which were the quickest and most serviceable solution to their need.

The long day passed and night closed in again. The crosses, carried down by the careful Baptiste, stood like a fence about the cabin, draped with fresh windflowers, with one gap left by which the men went to and fro on the way to logs they rolled to the river for the raft.

Johnson fell into heavy sleep and Cressey lay near him, smoking a last pipe. The old ivory-carver worked by the light of his oil lamp in the corner, although sunlight still shone in at the open window. The sled dogs had been brought and leashed inside the encircling crosses, but Cressey had scarcely dozed off when he heard their whimperings. Rising, he went outside.

From far off came the baying of the chase, and he saw the huntress flying down the ice, followed by her hounds. Johnson came from the cabin and both men stood in that twilight which had grown longer in in the waning summer that would soon give way to winter. A pale crescent moon danced on one silver toe, a fit companion for the lovely Diana dancing on the ice.

"Even now," said Johnson. "I can't believe but that she is a flesh and blood woman. Cressey, I'd like to clasp her hand and know for myself."

Cressey did not reply. The huntress was coming nearer, the baying of the hounds grew louder. He looked to see that the crosses were in place and did not observe that Johnson had stepped past them until he heard the cry of Baptiste. Then he saw the dark figure of the man, the radiant white fire of the huntress' beauty, as they melted into each other's arms. With a yell, Cressey leaped the barrier of crosses and raced to where the two stood swaying in close embrace.

As if the hounds sensed the symbol on Cressey's breast, they fell back as he approached. He had a swift wonder at their timidity until his hands seized Johnson, who screamed and writhed at his touch and fought being rescued as the huntress' head lifted from his shoulder and she slowly retreated, step by step, her moistened red lips parted, showing her strong white teeth in almost a snarl of hatred.

Cressey fought to draw Johnson to safety, and as he came nearer the cabin, the huntress advanced, hands reaching, weaving, tearing at the space separating her from her victim, unable to brush aside or combat the force for good protecting him. Slowly the hounds advanced with her, and the cries of the sled dogs made the night hideous, when suddenly the huntress threw back her head and shrilled her wild call.

Once inside the barrier of crosses, Cressey dropped the half-crazed Johnson into Baptiste's arms, then he stared into the brightening light of dawn on the mountains. There were sounds from far off, of crashing brush and thunderingly ominous tread, and into their view loomed the giant of the ancient world, lumbering forward with incredible speed until it reached the woman's side, a dreadful menace which only for the frail barrier could have crushed the cabin and scattered the last vestige of men and dogs.

The howling of sled dogs and cries of men were terror-muted for a few moments. Then they were alert. Guns cracked in sharp fusillade, but the ghost-beasts neither quivered nor showed signs of a wound. The huntress was screaming at her beasts and waving white arms to urge them on, but they slunk aside until she howled at the mammoth, who caught her in his trunk and swung her to his broad head. There she stood, ethereally lovely and evil, her lips stained by the interrupted draft of human life, while the night waned and the blessed sun shot from the curving breasts of snow on Mount Logan. A cry as of frenzied despair came from her. The mammoth turned, the hounds leaped ahead, and the whole cavalcade vanished in the direction of the ice-fields.

Cressey turned to find Johnson as mad as he had been.

"You cur," he howled, "to come between me and my woman. You've had your day and now you begrudge me my hour of happiness."

"Johnson, she killed Stamwell, drained his body of life. She almost killed me. Left me like a maniac, as she will leave you. Here, this trinket of Baptiste's protected me; you shall wear it."

He dropped the thong of the crucifix over Johnson's head and heard his cry of pain. Cressey knew the white-hot searing of that symbol on flesh accursed and felt only pity for the man. All that day Johnson moaned, watched over by Cressey, while Baptiste directed the men in their task of making the raft.

"No ghost can pass running water," he said, and that night the logs were lashed together and the rafts moored to shore trees, and the barrier of crosses was strengthened.

Meanwhile, working ceaselessly, Jo had cut the ivory from the feet of the huntress he was carving, and was chiseling her pretty toes with their filbert-shaped nails. He had truly caught the grace of her dancing poise in the slender ankles, and she stood like a fairy molded of mellow gold when the sun touched the far horizon and the brief night began in violet-tinted twilight.

Cressey was fascinated by the figure. "Tell Jo I must have it. I will pay well, five hundred dollars, even a thousand. I will take her out with me."

Reluctantly Baptiste interpreted his demand and for the first time the old ivory-carver showed emotion. Fire leaped to his eyes as he wrathfully waved Cressey aside and refused to consider even so great a sum of money for his statue of the woman.

Cressey did not argue, but in his heart he determined to obtain the ivory figure, and he fell asleep planning a means to that end. He slept lightly, dreaming of the huntress, and muttering in his sleep. His broken talk wakened Johnson, who looked toward Cressey with hatred in his eyes, which changed to cunning.

Johnson cautiously slipped the thong of the crucifix from his neck and it dropped to the floor. Then for a time he lay still, except for the convulsive twitching of his body and the rolling of his tortured eyes.

At midnight came the whimpering of the sled-dogs and the baying of white hounds from afar. Immediately every man in the cabin was alert. They grabbed guns and plunged outside, waiting that dread visitation. The moon was fuller and gave silver light pricked out by velvet dark blotches of the trees. The glacial river gleamed like pearl. Another day and the party would have escaped, afloat on rafts carried by the swift-running stream, but this one night must be endured

The huntress was not alone with her dogs, for she stood on the head of the mammoth as it thundered into the plain cleared by its voracious feeding, and about them raced the white hounds.

The hearts of the men were seized by icy fingers of fear even while they poured volley after volley of shots at the advancing horror and realized as they pulled the triggers that no man-invented mode of death could halt them.

The old ivory-carver, Jo, alone seemed fearless or careless of those terrible ghouls of eld, for he came leisurely from the cabin, toddling toward the barrier fence of wooden crosses and peering as if to feast his sight on the vision he had foregone during those nights he toiled at the ivory figure of the woman.

Cressey stepped to Jo's side. He had forgotten Johnson in the cabin. There was none to see Johnson spring from the couch and with the desperation of a madman seize the ivory huntress in his arms and rush from the door on shoeless feet that made no sound.

Cressey's first glimpse of him came when Johnson leaped the barrier of crosses and headed for the river raft. But the huntress had already seen that plunging human and her cry rang like the long-drawn note of a silver horn. The mammoth lunged forward, the hounds leaped in white arcs of flying fur, and Johnson's scream stabbed through the din of animal howls.

They saw the huntress leap from her titanic steed to catch Johnson in her arms; saw the ivory figure knocked from his grasp. The golden hair of the huntress enveloped him like a ruddy silk mantle and her mouth was pressed to his throat.

But a greater tragedy was imminent. As if the scent of human blood maddened it, the mammoth plunged forward, its great tusks lunging between the leaping hounds to stab its human enemy; and the hounds closed in with unearthly helpings.

Transfixed by the sight, the men at the cabin stared at the calamity they were powerless to avert, until there came a loud crunch as the mammoth's foot trod on the ivory figure of the huntress which Johnson had dropped.

Then, as if at a signal, the ghost-beasts seemed frozen in their tracks, and from them came a glistening white mist that swayed to and fro as it rose and drifted across the face of the young moon, and the watchers saw, like a frail cloud, the shining form of that lovely, hell-born huntress as it blew away on the wind of dawn.

Light grew swiftly. The sun came up and shone on a mountainous mass of hairy mammoth flesh and long-furred hounds lying on the tundra.

As they stood, chained to the spot by a paralysis of horror, every nerve taut, the men at the cabin saw that mound of flesh subside to pulp, and a dreadful stench arose in a smoky steam. By noon there was a gelatinous mass, which by nightfall had soaked into the earth, leaving only the skeletons. A clean cold wind from the snows sweetened the air where Jo prodded the bones with a stick to recover all that was left of his ivory huntress, a head on which the features faithfully depicted her inscrutable smile, with lips and teeth slightly parted.

Cressey did not offer to buy it, and the head still hangs above Jo's cabin door. One glance at that lovely face had power to recall all too vividly the fate of Stamwell and Johnson, for whom crosses were erected in the valley and lop-sticks carved with their names. Cressey did not smile nor dispute the assertion of Baptiste that he should never return to that valley.

"M'sieu," said Baptiste, "dat devil-womans have dreenk your blood wan time, an' eef some day she come back, she catch you again, because all womans ees jealous, an' eef a womans git jealous eet open doors of ver' bad hells. You do what Baptiste say, you wear a l'il crucifix all time." And though not a religious man, Cressey has never since been without that symbol.

Jorgas

Robert Nelson

Robert Nelson

Robert Nelson was a young Illinois fan of Weird Tales *who sold the magazine several unusual poems before his death at age seventeen. Nelson was a fan of Clark Ashton Smith's poetry, and his work reflects the strong influence of that writer.*

Jorgas

Robert Nelson

With sighs the potioned flowers stooped to kiss
Pale Jorgas just awaking from his dream
Of olent wine and swirling-shadowed bliss,
And as the blue mist crawled upon the glade
The flowers talked and sang to him, and swayed
In shades with his, but all at once did scream,
"O Jorgas, why art thou a saddened man?"
"My thoughts are wildly blown with lunar dust,
My lips, wine-steeped, are sore from evil prongs,
I cannot break the thousand dream-wrought thongs
That trammel me with dreadful death and must."
"O Jorgas, wine...perfumes...no courtezan? . . .
"Oh, cease, and leave me to my misery.
What poisoned hand is this that smooths a face
Of bronze and plucks thy bitter petals free?"
"O Jorgas, wine and shadows all embrace
Themselves with us and thee in ecstacy."
"No! no! I see...I hear ...my eyes...that glare..."
"Pale one, look up ... Her palm... Her heart... laid bare...
Take it, and She an orb will give to thee..."
"No! no! it is accurst! I know...I know
The vipers three who kissed and nuzzled it..."
"You dream as One who dreams below the Pit."
"I would let the flames to wrestle with the snow—"
"No, stay—take thou this knife and cut in twain
The throat of Him who offered thee domain
Within the realm where Specters laugh and dwell."
"Oh, do not say—what is there I can gain?
No! no! I would rather dream in silent hell...."
"He tramps on skulls and gluts on matted hair.
He comes—the Thing, whose noisome cerements shed,
Reveal the storm, the dead, in tortured tread.
O Jorgas, fare thee well! We die in prayer."
"Jorgas, I am He who comes in burning sod."
"My mind betrayed! Oh, do not slay me now!
Remove thy long-dead face and burnt-off brow—"
"Jorgas! Beat thy evil breast and cry for God!"